RUTH FIELDING AT THE WAR FRONT; OR, THE HUNT FOR THE LOST SOLDIER
BY
Alice B. Emerson

RUTH FIELDING AT THE WAR FRONT; OR, THE HUNT FOR THE LOST SOLDIER

Published by Silver Scroll Publishing

New York City, NY

First published circa 1990

Copyright © Silver Scroll Publishing, 2015

All rights reserved

Except in the United States of America, this book is sold subject to the condition that it shall not, by way of trade or otherwise, be lent, re-sold, hired out, or otherwise circulated without the publisher's prior consent in any form of binding or cover other than that in which it is published and without a similar condition including this condition being imposed on the subsequent purchaser.

ABOUT SILVER SCROLL PUBLISHING

Silver Scroll Publishing is a digital publisher that brings the best historical fiction ever written to modern readers. Our comprehensive catalogue contains everything from historical novels about Rome to works about World War I.

RUTH FIELDING AT THE WAR FRONT: CHAPTER I: TO GET ACQUAINTED

It was a midwinter day, yet the air was balmy. The trees were bare-limbed but with a haze clothing them in the distance that seemed almost that of returning verdure. The grass, even in mid-winter, showed green. A bird sang lustily in the hedge.

Up the grassy lane walked a girl in the costume of the active Red Cross worker—an intelligent looking girl with a face that, although perhaps not perfect in form, was possessed of an expression that was alluring.

Neither observant man nor woman would have passed her, even in a crowd, without a second glance. There was a cheerful light in her eye and a humorous curve to her not too-full lips that promised an uplifting spirit within her even in serious mood.

It seemed as though this day—and its apparent peace—must breed happiness, although it was but a respite in the middle of winter. The balmy air, the chirrup of the bird, the far-flung reaches of the valley which she could see from this mounting lane, all delighted the senses and soothed the spirit.

Suddenly, with an unexpectedness that was shocking, there was a tremor in the air and the echo of a rumbling sound beneath the girl's feet. The crack of a distant explosion followed. Then another, and another, until the sound became a continual grumble of angry explosions, resonant and threatening.

The girl did not stop, but the expression of her face lost its cheerfulness. The song of the bird was cut off sharply. It seemed as though the sun itself began drawing a veil over his face. The peaceful mood of nature was shattered.

The girl kept on her way, but she no longer stepped lightly and springily. Those muttering guns had brought a somber cloak for her feelings—to her very soul.

Somewhere a motor began to hum. The sound came nearer with great rapidity. It was a powerful engine. It was several seconds before the girl looked up instead of along the road in search of the seat of this whirring sound.

There shot into view overhead, and flying low, an aeroplane that looked like a huge flying insect—an enormous armored grasshopper. Only its head was somewhat pointed and there, fixed in the front, was the ugly muzzle of a machine gun. The airplane flew so low that she could see the details.

There were two masked men in it, one at the wheel, the other at the machine gun. The aeroplane swooped just above her head, descending almost to the treetops, the roaring of it deafening the girl in the Red Cross uniform. There was the red, white and blue shield of the United States painted upon the underside of the car.

Then it was gone, mounting higher and higher, until, as she stood to watch it, it became a painted speck against the sky. That is the lure of the flying machine. The wonder of it—and the terror—attracts the eye and shakes the spirit of the beholder.

With a sigh the girl went on up the lane, mounting the hill steadily, on the apex of which, among giant forest trees, loomed the turrets and towers of a large chateau.

Again the buzzing of a motor broke the near-by stillness, while the great guns boomed in the distance. The sudden activity on the front must portend some important movement, or why should so many flying machines be drawn toward this sector?

But in a minute she realized that this was not an aeroplane she heard. Debouching into sight from the fringing thickets came a powerful motor car, its forefront armored. She could barely see the head and shoulders of the man behind the steering wheel.

Down the hill plunged the car, and the girl quickly stepped to the side of the lane and waited for it to pass. The roar of its muffler was deafening. In a moment she saw that the tonneau of the gray car was filled with uniformed men.

They were officers in khaki, the insignia of their several grades scarcely distinguishable against the dull color of their clothing. How different from the gay uniforms of the French Army Corps, which, until of late, the girl of the Red Cross had been used to seeing in this locality.

Their faces were different, too. Gray, lean, hard-bitten faces, their eyebrows so light and sparse that it seemed their eyes were hard stones which never seemed to shift their straight-ahead gaze. Yet each man in the tonneau and the orderly beside the driver on the front seat saluted the Red Cross girl as she stood by the laneside.

In another half-minute the car had turned at the bottom of the hill and was out of sight.

She sighed again as she plodded on. Now, indeed, was the spring gone from her limbs and her expression was weary with a sadness that, although not personal, was heavy upon her.

Her thought was with the aeroplane and the motor car and with the thundering guns at the battle front, not many miles away. Yet she hastened her steps up this grassy lane toward the chateau, in quite the opposite direction.

The sudden stir of the military life of this sector portended something unusual. An advance of the enemy or an attempt to make a drive upon the Allies' works. In any case, down in the little, low-lying town behind her, there might be increased need of hospital workers. She must, before long, be once more at the hospital to meet the first ambulances rolling in from the field hospitals or from the dressing stations at the very front.

She reached the summit of the ridge, over which the lane passed to the valley on the west side of the hill. The high arch of the gateway of the chateau was in sight.

Coming from that direction, walking easily, yet quickly, was the lean military figure of a young man who switched the roadside weed stalks with a light cane. He looked up quickly as the girl approached, and his rather somber face lighted as though the sight of her gave him pleasure.

Yet his gaze was respectful. He was handsome, keenly intelligent looking and not typically French, although he was dressed in the uniform of a branch of the French service, wearing a major's chevrons. As the Red Cross girl came nearer, he put his heels together smartly, removed his kepi, and bowed stiffly from the waist. It was not a Frenchman's bow.

The girl responded with a quiet bend of her head, but she passed him by without giving him any chance to speak. He followed her only with his eyes—and that but for a moment; then he went on down the lane, his stride growing momentarily longer until he passed from view.

A cry from the direction of the broad gateway ahead next aroused the attention of the girl in the

Red Cross uniform. She looked up to see another girl running to meet her.

This was a short, rather plump French girl, whose eyes shone with excitement, and who ran with hands outstretched to meet those of the Red Cross girl. The latter was some years the older.

"Oh, Mademoiselle Ruth! Mademoiselle Ruth Fielding!" cried the French girl eagerly. "Did you meet him? Ah-h!"

Ruth Fielding laughed as she watched the mobile face of her friend. The latter's cheeks were flushed with excitement, her eyes rolled. She was all aquiver with the emotion that possessed her.

"Did you see him?" she repeated, as their hands met and Ruth stooped to press her lips to the full ones of her friend.

"Did I see whom, you funny Henriette?" asked Ruth.

"Am I fon-nay?" demanded Henriette Dupay, in an English which she evidently struggled to make clear. "Then am I not nice?"

"You are both funny and nice," declared Ruth Fielding, hugging the girl's plump body close to her own, as they walked on slowly to the chateau gate. "Tell me. Who was I supposed to see? A motor full of officers passed me, and an aeroplane over my head——"

"Oh, non! non!" cried Henriette. Then, in awe: "Major Marchand."

"Oh! Is that Major Marchand?"

"But yes, Mademoiselle Ruth. Ah-h! Such a man—such a figure! He is Madame the Countess' younger son."

"So I understand," Ruth said. "He is safely engaged in Paris, is he not?" and her tone implied much.

"Ye-es. So it is said. He—he must be a ve-ry important man, Mademoiselle, or his duty would not keep him there."

"Unless the Boches succeed in raiding Paris from the air he is not likely to get hurt at all—this Major Marchand?"

"Oh!" pouted Henriette. "You are so critical. But he is—what you say?—so-o beautiful!"

"Not in my eyes," said Ruth grimly. "I don't like dolly soldiers."

"Oh, Mademoiselle Ruth!" murmured the French girl. "Do not let Madame the Countess suspect your feelings toward her younger son. He is all she has now, you know."

"Indeed? Has the older son fallen in battle?"

"The young count has disappeared," whispered Henriette, her lips close to Ruth's ear. "We heard of it only lately. But it seems he disappeared some months ago. Nobody knows what has become of him."

"He, at least, was on the battle front?" asked the American girl. "He is missing? Probably a prisoner of the Germans?"

"No-o. He was not at the front," confessed the other girl. "He, too, was engaged in Paris, it is understood. But hush! We are at the gate. I will ring. Don't, Mademoiselle Ruth, let the dear countess suspect that you do not highly approve of her remaining son."

The Red Cross girl smiled rather grimly, but she gave the promise.

CHAPTER II: AT THE CHATEAU

The two girls, arm in arm, approached the postern gate beside the wide iron grille that was never opened save for the passage of horses or a motor car. There was a little round shutter in the postern at the height of a man's head; for aforetime the main gateway had been of massive oak, bolt-studded and impervious to anything less than cannon shot. The wall of masonry that surrounded the chateau was both high and thick, built four hundred years or so before for defence.

An old-fashioned rope-pull hung beside the postern. Henriette dragged on this sharply, but the girls could not hear the tongue of the bell, for it struck far back in the so-called offices of the chateau, where the serving people had had their quarters before these war times had come upon the earth.

Now there were but few servants remaining at the chateau. For the most part the elderly Countess Marchand lived alone and used but few of the rooms.

As the girls waited an answer to their summons, Henriette said, in reference to what had already passed in conversation between them:

"It hurts me, dear friend, that anybody should doubt the loyalty of our countess whom we know to be so good. Why! there are people even wicked enough to connect her with that—that awful Thing we know of," and the girl dropped her voice and looked suddenly around her, as though she feared an unseen presence.

"As though she were a werwolf," she added, with a shudder.

"Pooh!" and Ruth Fielding laughed. "Nobody in their senses would connect Madame la Countess with such tales, having once seen her."

She thought now, as they waited, of her first visit to the chateau, and of the appearance of the Countess Marchand in her bare library. Whatever her sons might be—the young count who was missing, or this major whom she had just met in the grassy lane—Ruth Fielding was confident that the lady of the chateau was a loyal subject of France, and that she was trusted by the Government.

Ruth had called here herself on that occasion with a secret agent, Monsieur Lafrane, to clear up the mystery of a trio of criminals who had come from America to prey upon the Red Cross. These crooks had succeeded in robbing the Supply Department of the Red Cross, in which Ruth herself was engaged. But in the end they had fallen into the toils of the French secret service and Ruth had aided in their overthrow.

All this is told in the volume of this series immediately preceding our present story, entitled: "Ruth Fielding in the Red Cross; or, Doing Her Best for Uncle Sam." This was the thirteenth volume of the Ruth Fielding Series.

Of the twelve books that have gone before that only a brief mention can be made while Ruth and the young French girl are waiting for an answer to the bell.

At first we meet Ruth Fielding as she approaches Cheslow and the Red Mill beside the Lumano River, where Uncle Jabez, the miserly miller, awaits her coming in no pleasant frame of mind. He is her only living relative and he considers little Ruth Fielding a "charity child." She is made to feel this by his treatment and by the way in which the girls in the district school talk of her.

Ruth makes three friends from the start, however, who, in their several ways, help her to endure her troubles. One is Aunt Alvirah Boggs, who is nobody's relation but everybody's aunt, and whom Jabez Potter, the miller, has taken from the poorhouse to keep his home tidy and comfortable. Aunt Alvirah sees the good underlying miserly Uncle Jabez's character when nobody else can. She lavishes upon the little orphan girl all the love and affection that she would have given to her own children had she been blessed with any.

Ruth's other two close friends were the Cameron twins, Helen and Tom, the children of a wealthy storekeeper who lived not far from the Red Mill. The early adventures of these three are all related in the first book of the series, "Ruth Fielding of the Red Mill."

One virtue of Uncle Jabez's, which shines as brightly in his rather gloomy character as a candle in the dark, is that he always pays his debts. If he considers he owes anybody anything he is not satisfied until he pays it. Therefore, when Ruth recovers some money which had been stolen from him, he is convinced that it is only right for him to pay her tuition for at least a year at Briarwood Hall, where she goes to school with Helen Cameron, while Tom goes to a boy's boarding school called Seven Oaks.

The girls and Tom and his friends often got together for good times during their school years, and, in successive volumes, we meet them in winter adventures in the Northern woods at Snow Camp; in the summer at Lighthouse Point; in Wyoming at Silver Ranch; in lakeside and woodsy adventures on Cliff Island; enjoying most exciting weeks at Sunrise Farm, where Ruth wins a reward of five thousand dollars in aiding in the recovery of a pearl necklace stolen by the Gypsies. There are volumes, too, telling of the serious loss by fire of a dormitory building at Briarwood and how Ruth Fielding rebuilt it by the production of a moving picture; of her vacation down in Dixie; of her first year at Ardmore College, which she and Helen and several of her Briarwood chums entered; then of Ruth Fielding in the saddle when she went West again, this time for the production of a great picture entitled: "The Forty-Niners."

With the entrance into the war of the United States, Tom Cameron enlisted and went to France as a second lieutenant with the first Expeditionary Force. Ruth and Helen went into Red Cross work, leaving college before the end of their sophomore year for that purpose.

Ruth could not go as a nurse, but in the Supply Department she gained commendation and when a supply unit of the Red Cross was sent to France she went with it, while Helen went over with her father, who was on a commission to the front. Once there, the black-eyed girl found work to do in Paris while Ruth was enabled to be of use much nearer the front.

Indeed, at the opening of the present story the girl of the Red Mill is at work in the evacuation hospital at Clair, right behind a sector of the battle line that had been taken over by General Pershing's forces. Tom Cameron is with his regiment not many miles away. Indeed, his company might be engaged in this very activity that had suddenly broken out within sound, if not in sight, of Clair and the Chateau Marchand.

There was reason for Ruth Fielding's gravity of countenance—and grave it was, despite its natural cheerfulness of expression—for her interest in Tom Cameron and his interest in her had long been marked by their friends. Tom was in peril daily—hourly. It was no wonder that she revealed the ravages of war upon her mind.

"Sh!" whispered Henriette. "Here comes Dolge, the gardener. Now that Bessie is gone he is the oldest person Madame la Countess has in her employ."

"I wonder what became of Bessie. Monsieur Lafrane told me she was not apprehended with those men who helped her get away from the chateau."

"It is a mystery. She had served Madame so many years. And then—at the last—they say she was a spy for les Boches!"

Dolge appeared, with his toothless grin, at the round opening in the postern.

"The little Hetty and Mademoiselle l'Americaine," he mumbled. "Madame la Countess expects you."

He unchained the door and let them pass through. Then he shut and chained the door again just as though the chateau was besieged.

The girls did not wait for him. They walked up the curved avenue to the wide entrance to the great pile of masonry. The chateau was as large as a good-sized hotel.

Before the war there had been many comforts, Ruth understood, that now the countess was doing without. For instance, electric lights and some kind of expensive heating arrangement.

Now the lady of the chateau burned oil, or candles, like the peasants, and the chateau doors were wide open that the sun and air of this grateful day might help dry the tomb-like atmosphere of the reception hall.

"Ma foi!" said Henriette, commenting on this in a low voice, "even the beautiful old armor—the suits of mail that the ancient Marchands wore in the times of the Crusades—is rusty. See you! madame has not servants enough now to begin to care for the place."

"I suppose she has stored away the rugs and the books from the library shelves," began Ruth; but Henriette quickly said:

"Non! non! You do not understand, Mademoiselle, what our good lady has done. The wonderful rugs she has sold—that off the library floor, which, they say, the old count himself brought from Bagdad. And the books—all her library—have gone to the convalescent hospitals, or to the poilus in the trenches. For they, poor men, need the distraction of reading."

"And some of your neighbors suspect her," repeated Ruth thoughtfully.

"It is because of that awful Thing—the werwolf!" hissed Henriette.

Then there was time for no further speech. A middle-aged woman appeared, asked the girls in, and led the way to the library. A table was set near the huge open fireplace in which a cheerful fire crackled. On the table was a silver tea service and some delicate porcelain cups and saucers.

The kettle bubbled on the hob. Chairs were drawn close before the blaze, for, despite the "springiness" in the air without, the atmosphere in the vast library of the chateau was damp and chill.

As the girls waited before the fire a curtain at the end of the room swayed, parted, and the tall and plainly robed figure of the countess entered. She had the air of a woman who had been strikingly beautiful in her younger days. Indeed, she was beautiful still.

Her snowy hair was dressed becomingly; her cheeks were naturally pink and quite smooth, despite the countless wrinkles that netted her throat. The old lace at the neck of her gown softened her ivory-hued skin and made its texture less noticeable.

Her gown was perfectly plain, cut in long, sweeping lines. Nor did she wear a single jewel. She swept forward, smiling, and holding out her hand to Ruth.

"Here is our little Hetty," she said, nodding to the French girl, who blushed and bridled. "And Mademoiselle Fielding!" giving the latter a warm handclasp and then patting Henriette's cheek. "Welcome!" She put them at their ease at once.

The few family portraits on the walls were all the decorations of the room. The book cases themselves were empty. Madame la Countess made the tea. On the table were thin slices of war bread. There was no butter, no sugar, and no milk.

"We are learning much these days," laughed the countess. "I am even learning to like my chocolate without milk or cream."

"Oh!" And Henriette whipped from the pocket of her underskirt something that had been making her dress sag on that side. When she removed the wrappings she produced a small jar of thick yellow cream.

"My child! It is a luxury!" cried the countess. "I shall feel wicked."

"Perhaps it will be nice to feel wicked for once," Ruth said, feeling a little choke in her throat. She drew from concealment her own contribution to the "feast"—several lumps of sugar.

"Do not fear," she added, smiling. "None of the poor poilus are deprived. This is from my own private store. I wish there was more of it, but I can't resist giving a lump now and then to the village children. They are so hungry for it. They call me 'Mam'zelle Sucre'."

"And I would bring you cream often, Madame," Henriette hastened to add, "but our good old Lally died, you know, and the little cow does not give much milk as yet, and it is not as rich. Oh! if that werwolf had not appeared to us! You remember, Mademoiselle Ruth? Then old Lally died at once," and the French girl nodded her head vigorously, being fully convinced of the truth of the old superstition.

The countess flushed and then paled, but nobody but Ruth noticed this. The American girl watched her hostess covertly. The bare mention of a superstition that had the whole countryside by the throat, disturbed much the countess' self-control.

The next moment there was a step in the hall and then the door opened to admit the same young officer Ruth Fielding had met in the lane—Major Henri Marchand.

"Pardon, Maman," he said, bowing, and speaking to his mother quite like a little boy. "Do I offend?"

"Do come in and have a cup of tea, Henri. There is sugar and real cream—thanks to our two young friends here. You remember our petite Hetty, of course? And this is our very brave Mademoiselle Ruth Fielding, of the American Red Cross. My younger son, Monsieur Henri," the countess said easily.

Major Marchand advanced into the room promptly. To Henriette he bowed with a smile. Ruth put out her hand impulsively, and he bowed low above it and touched his lips to her fingers.

The girl started a little and glowed. The manner of his address rather shocked her, for she was unused to the European form of greeting. Henri's deep, purple eyes looked long into her own brown ones as he lingeringly released her hand.

"Mademoiselle!" he murmured. "I am charmed."

Ruth did not know whether she was altogether charmed or not! She felt that there was something rather overpowering in such a greeting, and she rather doubted the sincerity of it.

She could understand, however, little Henriette's sentimental worship of the young major. Henri Marchand was the type of man to hold the interest of most girls. His eyes were wonderful; his cheek as clear and almost as soft as a woman's; he wore his uniform with an air scarcely to be expressed in ordinary words.

Henriette immediately became tongue-tied. Ruth's experience had, however, given her ease in any company. The wonderful Major Marchand made little impression upon her. It was plain that he wished to interest the Americaine Mademoiselle.

The little tea party was interrupted by the appearance of Dolge at the library door.

"A young American in an ambulance inquires for Mademoiselle Fielding at the gate," said Dolge, cap in hand. "She is needed in haste, below there at the hospital."

CHAPTER III: A PERILOUS PROJECT

"That can be no other than Charlie Bragg," announced Ruth, getting up in haste, and naming a young friend of hers from the States who had been an ambulance driver for some months. "Something must have happened."

"I fear something is happening," Major Marchand said softly. "The sudden activity along this front must be significant, don't you think, Mademoiselle Fielding?"

Ruth's lips were pressed together for a moment in thought, and she eyed the major shrewdly.

"I really could not say," she observed coldly. Then she turned from him to take the hand of the countess.

"I'm sorry our little tea must be broken in upon," the American girl said.

She could not help loving the countess, no matter what some of the neighbors believed regarding her. But Ruth had her doubts about this son who was always in Paris and never at the front.

Henriette was too bashful to remain longer than Ruth, so she rose to go as well. The countess kissed her little neighbor and sent her favor to the girl's father and mother. Major Marchand accompanied the two visitors out of the chateau and toward the entrance gate, which Dolge had not opened.

"I sincerely hope we may meet again, Mademoiselle Fielding," the major said softly.

"That is not likely," she responded with soberness.

"No? Do you expect to leave Clair soon?"

"No," she said, and there was sharpness in her voice. "But I am much engaged in our hospital work—and you are not likely to be brought there, are you?"

Evidently he felt the bite in her question. He flushed and dropped his gaze. Her intimation was not to be mistaken. He seemed unlikely to be brought wounded to the hospital.

Before he could recover himself they were at the gate. Dolge opened the postern and the two girls stepped through, followed by the French officer. The young fellow in the American ambulance immediately hailed Ruth.

"Oh, I say, Miss Ruth!" he cried, "sorry to hunt you out this way, but you are needed down at the hospital."

"So I presume, or you would not have come for me, Charlie," she told him, smiling. "What is it?"

"Supplies needed for one of the field hospitals," he said. "And I tell you straight, Miss Ruth, they're in bad shape there. Not half enough help. The supply room of that station is all shot away—terrible thing."

"Oh, dear!" gasped Ruth. "Do you mean that the Germans have bombed it?"

"It wasn't an air raid. Yet it must have been done deliberately. They dropped a Jack Johnson right on that end of the hospital. Two orderlies hurt and the girl who ran the supply room killed. They want somebody to come right up there and arrange a new room and new stock."

"Oh! you won't go, Mademoiselle Ruth?" shrieked Henriette.

"It would be extremely dangerous," Major Marchand said. "Another shell might drop in the same place."

"Oh, we settled that battery. They tell me it's torn all to pieces. When our doughboys heard the Red Cross girl was killed they were wild. The gunners smashed the German position to smithereens. But it was awful for her, poor thing."

"The station needs supplies dreadfully, just the same," added Charlie Bragg. "And somebody who knows about 'em. I told the médicin-chef I'd speak to you myself, Miss Ruth——"

"I'll go with you. They can get along at Clair without me for a few days, I am sure."

"Good," returned Charlie, and moved over a little to make room on the seat for her. Major Marchand said:

"There must be something big going on over there. Is it a general advance, Monsieur?"

Ruth flashed him a look and laid her fingers gently on Charlie Bragg's arm. The ambulance driver was by no means dull.

"I can't say what is on foot," he said to the French officer. "I should think you might know more about it than I do," he added.

His engine began to rattle the somewhat infirm car. Charlie winked openly at Henriette, who laughed at him. The car began to move. Major Marchand stood beside the road and bowed profoundly again to Ruth—that bow from the hips. It was German, that bow; it proved that his military education had not been wholly gained in France.

She could not help doubting the loyalty of Major Henri Marchand as well as that of his older brother, the present count. Their mother might be the loveliest lady in the world, but there was something wrong with her sons.

Here the younger one was idling away his time about the chateau, or in Paris, so it was said, while the count had suddenly disappeared and was not to be found at all! Neither had been engaged in any dangerous work on the battle front. It was all very strange.

The bouncing ambulance was swiftly out of sight of the chateau gate. Ruth sighed.

"Say! isn't there anybody at all who can go with those supplies they're in need of but you, Miss Ruth?" inquired Charlie Bragg, looking sideways at her.

"No. I am alone at Clair, you know quite well, Charlie. The supplies are entirely under my care. I can teach somebody else over there at the bombed hospital in a short time how to handle the things. Meanwhile, the matron—or somebody else—can do my work here. It would not do to send a greenhorn to such a busy hospital as this must be to which you are taking me."

"Busy! You said it!" observed the driver. "You'll see a lot of rough stuff, Miss Ruth; and you haven't been used to that. What'll Tom Cameron say?" and he grinned suddenly.

Ruth laughed a little. "Every tub must stand on its own bottom, Aunt Alvirah says. I must do my duty."

"It'll be a mighty dangerous trip. I'm not fooling you. There are places on the road—— Well! the Boches are all stirred up and they are likely to drop a shell or two almost anywhere, you know."

"You came through it, didn't you?" she demanded pluckily.

"By the skin of my teeth," he returned.

"You're trying to scare me."

"Honest to goodness I'm not. They sent me over for the supplies and somebody to attend to them."

"Well?" she said inquiringly, as Charlie ceased to speak.

"But I didn't think you'd have to make the trip. Isn't there anybody else, Miss Ruth?" and the young fellow was quite earnest now.

"Nobody," she said firmly. "No use telling me anything more, Charlie. For the very reason the trip is dangerous, you wouldn't want me to put it off on somebody else, would you?"

He said no more. The car rattled down into the little town, with its crooked, paved streets and its countless smells. Clair was the center of a farming community, and, in some cases, the human inhabitants and the dumb beasts lived very close together.

The hospital sprawled over considerable ground. It was but two stories in height, save at the back, where a third story was run up for the "cells" of the nurses and the other women engaged in the work. Ruth ran up at once to her own tiny room to pack her handbag before she did anything else.

The matron met her at the supply-room door when she came down. She was a voluble, if not volatile, Frenchwoman of certain age.

"I dread having you go, Mademoiselle Ruth," she said, with her arm about the girl. "I feel as though you were particularly in my care. If anything should happen to you——"

"You surely would not be blamed," said Ruth, smiling. "Somebody must go and why not I? Please send two orderlies to carry out these boxes. This list calls for a lot of supplies. Surely the ambulance will be filled."

Which was, indeed, the case. When she finally went downstairs, turning the key of her storeroom over to the matron, the ambulance body was crowded with cases. The stretchers had been taken out before Charlie Bragg drove in. Ruth must occupy the seat beside him in front.

She did not keep him waiting, but ran down with her bag and crept in under the torn hood beside him. Several of the nurses stood in the door to call good-bye after her. The sentinel in the courtyard stood at attention as the car rolled out of the gate.

"Well," remarked Charlie Bragg, "I hope to thunder nothing busts, that's all. You've never been to the front, have you?"

"No nearer than this," she confessed.

"Humph! You don't know anything about it."

"But is the hospital you are taking me to exactly at the front?"

"About five miles behind the first dressing station in this sector. It's under the protection of a hill and is well camouflaged. But almost any time the Boches may get its range, and then—goodnight!"

With which remark he became silent, giving his strict attention to the car and the road.

CHAPTER IV: UNDER FIRE

The day was fading into evening as the car went over the first ridge and dropped out of sight of Clair and the sprawling hospital in which Ruth Fielding had worked so many weeks.

She felt that she had grown old—and grown old rapidly—since coming to her present work in France. She was the only American in that hospital, for the United States Expeditionary Forces had only of late taken over this sector of the battle line and no changes had been made in the unity of the workers at Clair.

They all loved Ruth there, from the matron and the surgeon-in-chief down to the last orderly and porter. Although her work was supposed to be entirely in the supply department, she gave much of her time to the patients themselves.

Those who could not write, or could not read, were aided by the American girl. If there was extra work in the wards (and that happened whenever the opposing forces on the front became active) Ruth was called on to help the nurses.

Thus far no American wounded had been brought into the Clair Hospital—a fact easily understood, as the entire force save Ruth was French. It would not be long, however, before the American Red Cross would take over that hospital and the French wounded would be sent to the base hospital at Lyse, where Ruth had first worked on coming to France.

Up to this very moment—and not an unexciting moment it was—Ruth Fielding had never been so far away from Clair in this direction. In the distance, as they mounted another ridge, she saw the flaring lights which she had long since learned marked the battle front. The guns still muttered.

Now and again they passed cavities where the great shells had burst. But most of these were ancient marmite holes and the grass was again growing in them, or water stood slimy and knee-deep, and, on the edges of these pools, frogs croaked their evensong.

There were not many farmhouses in this direction. Indeed, this part of France was "old-fashioned" in that the agricultural people lived in little villages for the most part and went daily to their fields to work, gathering at night for self-protection as they had done since feudal times.

Now and again the ambulance passed within sight of a ruined chateau. The Germans had left none intact when they had advanced first into this part of the country. They rolled through two tiny villages which remained merely battered heaps of ruins.

Orchards were razed; even the shade trees beside the pleasant roads had been scored with the ax and now stood gaunt and dead. Some were splintered freshly by German shells. As the light faded and the road grew dim, Ruth Fielding saw many ugly objects which marked the "frightfulness" of the usurpers. It all had a depressing effect on the girl's spirits.

"Are you hungry, Miss Ruth?" Charlie Bragg asked her at last.

"I expect I shall be, Charlie," she replied. "Our tea at the chateau was almost a fantom tea."

"Gosh! isn't it so?" he said slangily. "What these French folks live on would starve me to death. Mighty glad to have regular Yankee rations. But," he added, "we'll be too late to get chow when we come to the hospital, I am afraid. We'll try Mother Gervaise."

"Who is Mother Gervaise?" asked Ruth, glad to have some topic of conversation with the ambulance driver.

"She's an old woman who used to be cook at one of these chateaux here, they say. She'll feed us well for four francs each."

"Four francs!"

"Sure. Price has gone up," said Charlie dryly. "These French folk are bound to think that every American is a millionaire. And I don't know but it is worth it," and he grinned. "Think of being looked on as a John D. Rockefeller everywhere you go! I'd never rise to such a height in the States."

"No, I presume not," Ruth admitted with a laugh. "But how is it that this Mother Gervaise, as you call her, is not afraid to stay here?"

"She stays to watch the gold grow in her stocking," Charlie replied, shrugging his shoulders almost as significantly as a Frenchman.

"Oh! Is she that much of a miser?"

"You've said it. She stayed when the Germans first came and fed them. When they retreated she stayed and met the advancing British (the French did not come first) with hot soup, and changed her price from pfennigs to shillings. Get her to tell you about it. It is worth listening to—her experience."

Charlie Bragg stopped the car suddenly and got out. Ruth looked ahead with curiosity. The road seemed rather smooth and quite unoccupied. There was a group of trees, tortured by gunfire, which hid a turn in the track and what lay beyond. Charlie was tinkering with the engine of the machine.

"What is the matter?" Ruth ventured to ask.

"Nothing—yet," he returned. "But we've got to get around that next turn in a hurry."

"Why?"

"It's a wicked corner," said Charlie. "I might as well tell you—then you won't squeal if anything happens."

"Oh! Do you think I am a squealer?" she demanded rather tartly.

"I don't know," and he grinned again. He was an imp of mischief, this Charlie Bragg, and she did not know how to take him.

"You're not 'spoofing me,' as our British brothers put it?"

"It's an honest-to-goodness bad corner—especially at night," Charlie returned quite seriously now. "Boches know we fellows have to use it——"

"You mean the ambulances?"

"Yep. They spot us. We run without lights, you know; but every once in a while they drop a shell there. They have the range perfectly. They caught one of my bunkies there only a week ago."

"Oh, Charlie! An American?"

"No. Scotch. Only Scotty in this section, and a mighty nice fellow. Well, he'll never drive that boat again."

"Oh!" gasped Ruth. "Was he killed?"

"Shucks! No!" scoffed Charlie. "But his ambulance was smashed to bits. Luckily he hadn't any load with him at the time. But it would have been all one to the Boches."

Bragg got in beside the girl again, tried out his levers, and suddenly shot the car ahead.

"Hang on!" cried Charlie Bragg under his breath.

The ambulance shot down to the corner. It was all black shadow there, and, as Charlie intimated, he dared use no lights. If there was an obstruction they would crash into it!

The dusk had fallen suddenly. The sky was overcast, so not a star flecked the firmament. Through the gloom the ambulance raced, the young fellow stooping low over the steering wheel, trying to peer ahead.

How many hundreds of times had he made similar runs? Ruth had never before appreciated just what it meant to be driving an ambulance through these roads so near the battle front.

For five minutes a heavy gun had not spoken. Suddenly the horizon ahead lit up with a broad white flare. There came the resonant report of a huge gun—so distant that Ruth knew it could be nothing but a German Bertha.

Almost instantly the whine of a shell was audible—coming nearer and nearer! Ruth Fielding, cowering on the seat of the automobile, felt as though the awful missile must be aimed directly at her!

The car shot around the curve where the broken trees stood. With a yell like that of a lost soul—a demon from the Pit—the shell went over their heads and exploded in the grove.

The ambulance was spattered with a hail that might have been shrapnel, or stones and gravel—Ruth did not know. The hood sheltered her. She was on the far side of the seat, anyway.

And then, with a shout of warning, Charlie shut down and tried to stop the car within its own length. Ruth saw a hole yawning before them—a pit in the very middle of the road.

"They've dropped one here since I came along!" yelled the young man, just as the ambulance pitched, nose first, into the cavity.

They were stalled. Suppose the Boches sent another shell hurtling to this spot? They were likely to be wiped out in a breath.

CHAPTER V: MOTHER GERVAISE

Neither Ruth nor the driver was thrown out of the stalled ambulance. But Charlie jumped out in a hurry and held out his hand to the girl.

"You got to beat it away from here, Miss Ruth," he urged. "Another of those shells is likely to drop any minute. Hurry!"

Ruth had no desire to stay at that perilous corner of the road; but when she started away from the stalled car she found that she was alone.

"Aren't you coming, Charlie Bragg?" she demanded, turning back.

"Go on! Go on!" he urged her. "I've got to get this old flivver out of the mud. Keep right on to a little house you'll see on the left under the bank. Don't go past it in the dark. That's Mother Gervaise's cottage. It's out of reach of the Boches' shells."

"But you'll be killed, Charlie Bragg!" wailed the girl, suddenly realizing all the peril of their situation.

"Haven't ever been killed yet," he returned. "I tell you I've got to get this flivver out of the hole. These supplies have got to be taken to that field hospital. They're needed. I can't leave 'em here and run."

"But you expect me to run!" burst out Ruth, in sudden indignation.

"You can't help here. No use your taking a chance. You'll be in enough danger later. Now, you go on, Miss Ruth. Scoot! Here comes another!"

They heard the whine of the flying shell almost on top of the thud of the distant gun. Charlie seized her hand and they ran up the road for several yards. Then he stopped short, as the shell burst—this time far to the left of the stalled ambulance.

"Gosh!" he exclaimed. "You've got me rattled, too. Here! I'll go along to Mother Gervaise with you. Some of the fellows may be there and I can get help. Come on."

"Oh, Charlie!" murmured the girl. "I'm afraid for you."

"Trying to make me a quitter, are you?" he demanded. "Don't you know that if the Boches get you, they get you, and that's all there is to it? And one way or another that fliver's got to be got out of that hole."

Ruth was silenced. This young fellow—"boy" he called him in her own mind—had a quality of courage that shamed her. It was just the kind of bravery needed for the work he was doing in the war—a measure of recklessness that keeps one from counting the cost too exactly. Charlie Bragg had a philosophy of his own that kept him cheerful in the face of peril and was eminently practical at just this time.

He hurried her along the road, his hand under her elbow, seemingly able to see in the dark like a cat. But it was all black before Ruth's eyes, and she stumbled more than once. Her knees felt weak.

"I—I am scared, Charlie," she confessed, almost in a whisper.

"Yep. So was I, at first. But you know a fellow can't give in to it. If he does he'll never get to be a first-class ambulance driver. I bet some of the boys will be here at Mother Gervaise's and I can get help."

Another moment, and they seemed to turn a corner in the road and Ruth saw a small patch of light at the left of the roadway. She made it out to be an open window—the swinging shutter flung back against the wall. There was no glass in the opening.

"There it is," Charlie said. "You might have passed it right by, alone. You see, the house is close up against the high bank, and the hill is between us and the front. The Boches can't drop a shell here. It's a regular wayfarer's rest. There's a car—and another. We'll be all right now."

Ruth saw the outlines of the two cars parked beside the road. The young fellow led her directly toward the patch of yellow lamplight. She saw finally a broad, thatched cottage, the eaves of the high-peaked roof almost within reach as they came to the door.

Charlie Bragg knocked, then, without waiting for a summons to enter, lifted the wooden latch and shoved the sagging door open.

"Hello, folks!" he said. "Got shelter for a couple of babes in the woods? I got stalled down there at the Devil's Corner, and—— Let me introduce Miss Fielding. She's real folks like ourselves."

He had pushed Ruth in and entered behind her. Two young men—plainly Americans—rose from the table where they were eating. A squarely built woman bent over the fire at the end of the room. She did not look around from her culinary task.

"Hello, Bragg!" was the response from the other ambulance drivers.

"Cub Holdness and Mr. Francis Dwyer," said Charlie, introducing the two. "I've got stalled, fellows."

He swiftly told of the accident and the two young men left the table. The Frenchwoman turned and waddled toward the table, stirring spoon in hand and volubly objecting.

"Non, non!" she cried. "You would spoil the so-good ragout. If you do not eat it while it is hot——"

"The ragout can be heated over," put in Charlie. "But if the Boches get my car with a shell—good-night! Come on, fellows. And bring a rope. I believe we three can pull the old girl out."

The boys tramped out of the cottage. Mother Gervaise turned to Ruth and stared at her with very bright, black eyes.

She was a broad-faced woman, brown and hearty-looking, and with a more intelligent appearance than many of the peasants Ruth had seen. She wore sabots with her skirt tucked up to clear her bare ankles. Her teeth were broad and strong and white, and she showed them well as she smiled.

"The mademoiselle is Americaine?" she said. "Like these ambulanciers? Ah! brave boys, these. And mademoiselle is of the Croix Rouge, is it not?"

"I am working in the hospital at Clair," Ruth told her. "I am on my way with supplies to a station nearer the front."

"Ma foi!" exclaimed Mother Gervaise. "This has been a bad business. You will sup, Mademoiselle, yes?"

"I will, indeed. The accident has not taken away my appetite."

"Isn't it so? We must eat, no matter what next happens," said the woman. "Me, now! I am alone. My whole family have been destroyed. My husband and his brother—both have been killed. I had no children. Now I think it is as well, for children are not going to have much chance in France for years to come. All my neighbors have scattered, too."

"Then you have always lived here? Even before the war?" Ruth asked.

"Oui, Mademoiselle. Always. I was born right in that corner yonder, on a straw pallet. The best bed my mother had. We have grown rich since those days," and she shrugged her shoulders.

"I was an only child and the farm and cot came to me. Of course, I had plenty of the young men come to make love to me and my farm. I would have none of that kind. Some said I went through the wood and picked up a crooked stick after all. But Pierre and me—ma foi! We were happy, even if the old father and Pierre's brother must come here to live, too.

"The old father he die before the Germans come. I thank le bon Dieu for that. Pierre and his brother were mobilized and gone before the horde of les Boches come along this road. I am here alone, then. I begin making coffee and soup for them. Well, yes! They are men, too, and become hungry and exhausted. I please them and they treat me well. I learn what it means to make money—cash-money; and so I stay. Money is good, Mademoiselle.

"I might have wished poison into their soup; but that would not have killed them. And had I doctored it myself I would have been hung, and been no better off. So I made friends," and she smiled grimly.

"But I learned how boastful men could be—especially Germans. One—he was a major and one of the nobility—stayed here overnight. He promised to take me back to Germany when the war was over—which would be in a few weeks. They were to be in Paris in a few days then.

"He promised I would be proud when I became all German. France, he said, would never be a separate country again. For most of the people—my people—he said, were weaklings. They would emigrate to America and the remaining would intermarry with Germans. So all France would become Germany.

"When he was awake, he was full of bombast, that major! When he was asleep he snored outrageously. Ugh! For the first time in my life I hate anybody," declared Mother Gervaise, shuddering.

"But he paid me well for his lodging. And his men paid me for the soup. They marched past steadily for two days. Then they were gone and the country all about was peaceful for a week. At the end of that time they come back."

Here Mother Gervaise smiled, but it was a victorious smile. Her face lighted up and her eyes shone again.

"Pellmell back they came," she repeated. "It was a retreat. Many had lost their guns and their packs. I had no soup for them. I said I had lost my poulets and all. But it was not so. I had them hidden.

"The orderly of my major came in here, threw up his hands, and shouted: 'No Paris! No Paris!' And then he tramped on with his fellows. They chopped the trees and blew up many houses. But mine was marked, as the Boches did in those first days: 'These are good people. Let them be.' So

I was not molested," finished Mother Gervaise.

"Now, sit you down, Mademoiselle, at the table. Here where I have spread a napkin. The ragout——

"Bless us and save us!" she added, as a sudden roar of voices sounded outside the cot and the throaty rattle of a motor engine. "Whom have we here?"

She went to the door and flung it open. Ruth hesitated at the chair in which she had been about to be seated. Outside she saw bunched several uniformed men. They were hilariously pushing into the cottage, thrusting the excited Mother Gervaise aside.

CHAPTER VI: THE MYSTERY

Ruth Fielding's rising fear was quenched when she saw the faces of the newcomers more clearly. They were those of young men belonging to the American Expeditionary Forces, as their uniforms betrayed. And they were teasing Mother Gervaise in the free and easy way of American youth.

Nor was she anywhere near as angry as she assumed. They pushed her into the cottage and crowded in themselves before they saw Ruth standing at the end of the long table. Then, quite suddenly, their voices fell.

Not so Mother Gervaise. She fetched one of her tormentors a sharp smack with the palm of her hand.

"Un vaurien!" she cried, meaning, in the slang of the day, "good-for-nothing." "You would take my house by storm! Do you think it is a Boche dugout you charge when you come to Mother Gervaise?"

The silence of the rough and careless fellows was becoming marked. Already the Frenchwoman was noticing it. She turned, saw their eyes fixed upon Ruth, and remarked:

"Ha! It's well they respect the mademoiselle. Come in, wicked ones, and shut the door."

Ruth, relieved, saw that all were young commissioned officers—a very, very young captain, two first lieutenants, and several subalterns. They bowed rather bashfully to Ruth, and could not take their eyes off her.

One finally said: "You must be the lady at the Clair Hospital—Miss Fielding? You're the only American girl at that station."

"I am Miss Fielding," Ruth returned. Her eyes shone, her tone grew softer. She saw that he belonged to Tom Cameron's regiment. "I have a friend in your regiment—Mr. Cameron. Lieutenant Thomas Cameron. Is he on duty with you?"

Their respectful silence when they tumbled in and saw her was marked. But the utter dumbness that followed this question was so impressive that Ruth could almost hear her own heart beat.

"What—— He is not hurt?" she cried, looking from one to the other.

"I believe not, Miss Fielding," the captain said. "He is not on duty with us. I can tell you nothing about Lieutenant Cameron."

The decision with which he spoke and the expression upon the faces of the others, appalled the girl. She could not find breath to ask another question.

Mother Gervaise bustled forward to set upon the napkin she had spread a plate of the ragout for Ruth. The latter sank into the chair. The young officers gathered upon the other side of the hearth. They were hopelessly dumb.

There was a noise outside—the chugging of a car. It was a welcome relief. The door opened again and Charlie Bragg and the other two boys entered.

"Well, the Boches didn't get us that time," said Charlie, with satisfaction. "Nor the old fliver, either. Hello! Here's General Haig and all his staff. Or is it General Disorder? Hurry up with the Mulligan, Mother Gervaise—we've got to gobble and go."

He slipped into the seat next to Ruth, smiling at her. He was just a hungry, slangy boy. But those others——

Ruth could scarcely force the food down; but she determined to make a meal for her body's sake. She did not know what was before her—how much work, or how hard it would be, before she obtained another meal. She managed to ask:

"Is the car all right again, Charlie?"

"You can't bust it!" he declared enthusiastically. "The Britishers make all manner of fun of 'em. Call 'em 'mechanical fleas' and all that. But with a hammer, a monkey-wrench, and some bale-wire, a fellow can perform major and minor operations on a fliver in the middle of a garageless wilderness and come through all right when better cars are left for the junk department to gather up and salvage."

The other two ambulance drivers to whom Ruth had been introduced came to the table and finished their suppers, Mother Gervaise grumblingly dishing up more hot stew for them.

"It is for you and such as you I slave and slave," she said. "And what thanks do I get?"

"For la zozotte do you work, Mother," said one, laughing. "And who would want better thanks than money?"

But Ruth kissed the woman when she rose to depart. She believed Mother Gervaise was "tender under her rough skin," as is the saying.

The young officers had not come to the table while Ruth remained; nor did Charlie pay much attention to them. At least, he did not try to introduce them, and Ruth was glad of that.

There was something wrong. There was a mystery. Why should Tom Cameron's own associates act so oddly when his name was mentioned?

She merely bowed to the officers, but shook hands with Charlie's brother ambulanciers. There seemed to her something very wholesome and fine about these youths who drove the ambulances. They had—most of them—come to France and enlisted in their present employment before the United States got into the war at all.

She suspected that many of them were of that class known about their home neighborhoods as "that boy of Jones'," or "that Jackson kid." In other words, their overflow of animal spirits, or ambition, or whatever it was, had probably made them something of a trial to their neighbors, if not to their families.

Ruth began to see them in a sort of golden glow of heroism. They were the truer heroes because they denied this designation. Charlie grew red and gruff if she as much as suggested that he was doing anything out of the ordinary. Yet she knew he had written a book about his first year's experiences and his brother had found a publisher for it in New York. His share of the proceeds from that book was going to the Red Cross.

Into the ambulance they climbed, and again they were rolling over the dark and rough road. Ruth gathered together all her courage and asked:

"Do you know anything about Tom Cameron?"

"Tom Cameron?"

"Yes," she said. "I want to know what's happened to him, Charlie."

"For the love of Pete!" gasped the young fellow. "I didn't know anything had happened to him—again."

"I must know," Ruth told him, her voice quivering. "Some of those officers belonged to his battalion. All were of his regiment. But when I asked about him they refused to answer."

"You don't mean it!" Plainly Charlie Bragg was nonplussed. "I thought they acted funny," he said, with a sudden grin, which she sensed rather than saw. "But I thought it was girlitis. It has a terrible effect upon these fellows that haven't seen a real American girl for so long."

"I am serious, Charlie," she told him. "Something has happened to Tom—or about him. It seems to me that those officers were afraid to speak of it. As though there was something—something disgraceful about it!"

"Oh, say!" murmured Charlie. "That's not sense, you know."

"Of course Tom could do nothing disgraceful. But why should those men be afraid to speak of him?" cried the shaken girl. "He can't be wounded again. That can't be it. Haven't you heard a word?"

She suddenly realized that her companion had grown silent. He made no comment now upon her speech. She waited a full minute before bursting out again:

"You have heard something, Charlie! Something about Tom!"

"I—I don't know," he muttered. "I didn't know it was Tom."

"What is it?" she demanded with rising eagerness.

"I don't know that it's about Cameron now," he muttered. "I should hope not."

"Charlie Bragg! Do you want to drive me wild?" she demanded, clutching at his arm.

"Hold on! You'll have us in the ditch," he warned her.

"You answer me—at once!" she commanded.

"Oh—— But what can I say? I don't know anything. I don't believe Tom Cameron would be tricky—not a bit. And as for selling out to the Boches——"

"What do you mean?" almost shrieked the girl. "Are you crazy, Charlie Bragg?"

"There you go," he grumbled. "I told you I didn't know anything—for sure. But I heard some gossip."

"About Tom?"

"I didn't know it was about Tom. And I don't know now. But what you say about how funny those chaps acted——"

"Do explain!" begged Ruth. "Come right out with it, Charlie."

"Why, I heard a chap had been accused of giving information to the enemy. Yes. One of our own chaps—an American. It's said he met a Boche spy on listening post—right out there between the lines. He was seen twice."

"Not Tom?"

"No name told when I heard it. First a fellow saw him talking to a figure that stole away toward the German line. This fellow told his top sergeant, and toppy told his captain. They waited and watched. Three men saw the same thing happen. They were going to have the blamed traitor up before the brass hats when all of a sudden he disappeared."

"Who disappeared?" gasped Ruth Fielding.

"This chap they suspect gave information to the Boches. He's gone—like that!"

"Captured?" questioned Ruth breathlessly.

"Or gone over to them," returned Charlie, with evident unwillingness.

Ruth sighed. "But that never could be Tom Cameron!"

"You wouldn't think so," was the reply. "But that's all I can guess that those fellows had in mind when they would not answer you—good gracious, look at that!"

He braked madly. The ambulance rocked and came to an abrupt standstill. Across the track, scarcely two yards before the nose of the car, had dashed a white object, which, soundlessly, was gone in half a minute—swallowed up in the shadowy field beside the road.

"We see it again, Ruth," said Charlie Bragg, with a strange solemnity.

"What do you mean?" she demanded, but her voice, too, shook.

"The werwolf. That dog—whatever it is. Ghost or despatch-bearer, whatever you call it. I got a good sight of it again, Miss Ruth. Didn't you?"

CHAPTER VII: WHERE IS TOM CAMERON?

That the peasants of the surrounding territory should believe in that old and wicked legend of the werwolf was not to be considered strange. There is not a country in Europe where the tale of the human being who can change his form at will to that of a wolf, is not repeated.

Ruth Fielding had come across the superstition—and for the first time in the company of Charlie Bragg—as she had approached the town of Clair to begin her work in that hospital some months before.

This same white figure which they had both now glimpsed had crossed the road, flying as it was now toward the trenches. The werwolf, as the superstitious French peasants declared it to be, crossed both to and from the battle line; for it was frequently seen.

It was of this mystery Henriette Dupay had spoken in the library of the chateau that very afternoon. The Dupays believed absolutely in the reality of the werwolf.

Only, they were not of those who connected the "Thing" with the lady of the chateau. Although Ruth Fielding had reason to believe that the police authorities trusted the Countess Marchand and were sure of her loyalty, many of the peasants about the chateau believed that the werwolf was the unfortunate countess herself in diabolical form.

And even Ruth could not help feeling a qualm, as she saw the fast-disappearing creature—ghost or what-not—that fled into the darkness.

"Gosh!" murmured the slangy Charlie Bragg. "Enough to give a fellow heart-disease. I thought I was going to run it down."

"I wonder," said Ruth slowly, as he again started the car, "if it would not have been a good thing if you had run it down."

"Can't bust up a ghost that way, Miss Ruth," he returned, beginning to chuckle again.

"Talk sense, Charlie," she urged, forgetting for the moment the subject of the suspicion resting upon Tom Cameron and giving her mind to this other mystery. "You know, I've an idea this foolishness about a white wolf can be easily explained."

"Go ahead and explain," he returned. "I'm free to confess it's got me guessing."

"I believe it is the big greyhound, Bubu, that belongs to the Chateau Marchand. It is sent on errands to and from the frontier."

"Canine spy?" chuckled Charlie.

"I don't know just what he does. But I did think that the old serving woman, Bessie, that the countess brought with her from Mexico so many years ago, knew all about Bubu's escapades. But Bessie is not at the chateau now."

"Oh," said Charlie, "she was the woman who went off with those two crooks who helped your friend, Mrs. Rose Mantel, rob the Red Cross supply department."

"Not my friend, I should hope!" Ruth said sharply, for the matter Charlie touched upon was still a tender subject with the girl.

Her mind dwelt for a moment upon the presence of Major Henri Marchand at the chateau. He was there, and the greyhound, Bubu, was running at large again at night. Was there not something significant in the two facts? But she said nothing regarding this suspicion to the ambulance driver.

Instead, she came back to the subject which had occupied their minds previous to the appearance of the white object that had crossed the road.

"Of course, it is quite ridiculous," she said, "to think of Tommy Cameron doing anything at all treacherous. I can imagine his doing almost anything reckless, but always on the right side."

"Some little hero, is he?" chuckled Charlie Bragg.

"I think he is the stuff of which heroes are made—just like yourself, Charlie Bragg."

"Oh! I say!" he objected. "Now you are getting personal."

"Then don't try to be funny with me," declared Ruth earnestly. "I have too good an opinion of all our well-brought-up American boys—to which class both Tom and you belong—to believe that any of them could be made under any conditions to betray their fellows."

"Oh, as to that!" he admitted. "Nor any of our roughnecks, either. We've got a mighty fine army over here, rank and file. Deliberately, I doubt if any of them would give information to the Heinies. But they do say that when the Huns capture a man, if they want information, they don't care what they do to him to get it. The old police third degree isn't a patch on what these Boches do."

"I am not afraid that even torture would make Tom do anything mean," she said, with a little sob. "But these officers back there at that cottage must actually believe that he has gone over to the enemy."

"If Cameron is the fellow I heard about this morning," Charlie said gloomily enough, "it is generally believed that he has been two days beyond the lines—and he didn't have to go."

"Oh! Impossible!"

"I'm repeating what I heard. This flurry during the afternoon is an outcome of his disappearance. The German guns caught a train of ammunition camions and smashed things up pretty badly. Many tricks like that pulled off will make us mighty short of ammunition in this sector. Then Heinie can come over the top and do with us just as he pleases. Naturally, if the boys believe Cameron is at fault, they are going to be as sore on him as a boil."

"It would be utterly impossible for Tom to do such a thing!" the girl declared with finality.

Her assurance made the matter no less terrible. Ruth had no belief at all in Tom's willingly giving himself up to the enemy. Had there been a hundred witnesses to see him go, she would have denied the possibility of his being a traitor.

But she was very silent during the rest of that wild ride. Now and then they were stopped by sentinels and had to show their papers. At least, the Red Cross girl had to show hers. Charlie was pretty well known by everybody in this part of the war zone.

They would come to a dugout in the hillside, or a half-hidden hut, and be challenged by a sentinel, or by one of the military police. A pocket lamp would play upon Ruth's face, then upon her passport, and the sentinel would grunt, salute, and the car would plunge on again. It seemed to Ruth as though this went on for hours.

All the time her brain was active with the possibilities surrounding Tom Cameron's disappearance. What could really have happened to him? Should she write to Helen in Paris, or to his father in America, of the mystery? Indeed, would the censor let such news pass?

Once she had believed Tom seriously wounded, and for several days had hunted for him, expecting to find him mutilated. Fortunately her expectations at that time had been unfounded.

It seemed now, however, as though there could be no doubt but something very dreadful had happened to her friend. Added to his peril, too, was this awful suspicion that others seemed to hold regarding Tom's faithfulness.

It was going to be very hard, indeed, for Ruth Fielding to keep her mind on her work in the Red Cross while this uncertainty regarding Lieutenant Cameron remained.

CHAPTER VIII: THE CHOCOLATE PEDDLER

There was the flash of a lamp ahead.

"Here we are!" cried Charlie Bragg, in a tone of relief, bringing the car to a rocking stop.

Ruth Fielding could see but little as she looked out from under the hood of the ambulance. Yet she imagined there was a ridge of land behind the compound at the entrance to which they had halted.

Charlie got out and helped her down. A second man appeared in the gateway of the stockade beside the sentinel. The girl approached with the ambulance driver, who said:

"Here she is, Doc. And a load of stuff she says you'll need. This is Miss Fielding—and she's a regular good fellow. Doctor Monteith, Miss Fielding."

"I am glad to see you," the surgeon said warmly, taking the bag from Ruth and seizing her cold hand in his warm clasp. "We are very busy here and very short of supplies. Our stores were utterly destroyed when——"

He did not finish his statement, but ushered her into the compound. There were a few twinkling lights. She saw that there were a number of huts within this enclosure, each being, of course, a ward.

They left Charlie Bragg and an orderly to remove the supplies from the ambulance while the surgeon took Ruth to the hut that was to be her own. On the way they passed a crushed and shapeless mass that might once, the girl thought, have been another hut.

"Is that——?" she asked, pointing.

"Yes. The shell dropped squarely on it. We got her out from under the wreckage after putting out the fire. She was killed instantly," said the surgeon. "You are not frightened, Miss Fielding?"

"Why—yes," she said gravely. "I have, however, been frightened before. We have had night air raids at Clair. But, as Charlie Bragg says, 'I have not been killed yet.'"

"That is the way to look at it," he said cheerfully. "It's the only way. Back in all our minds is the expectation of sudden death, I suppose. Only—if it is sudden! That is what we pray for—if it is to come."

"I know," Ruth said softly. "But let us keep from thinking of it. Who is this lady?" she asked a moment later.

"Ah!" said the gentlemanly surgeon, seeing the figure in the doorway of the new supply hut. "It is our matron, Mrs. Strang. A lovely lady. I will leave you to her kindness."

He introduced the girl to the elderly woman, who examined Ruth with frank curiosity as she entered the hut.

"You are a real American, I presume," the woman said, smiling.

"I hope so."

"Not to be frightened by what has happened here already?"

"We expect such sad happenings, do we not?"

"Yes. We must. But this was a terrible thing. They say," the matron observed, "that it was the result of treachery."

"Oh! You do not mean——?"

"They say a man has sold a map of this whole sector to the Boches. A man—faugh! There are such creatures in all armies. Perhaps there are more among our forces than we know of. They say many of foreign blood among the Expeditionary Force are secretly against the war and are friends of the enemy."

"I cannot believe that!" cried Ruth. "We are becoming tainted with the fears of the French. Because they have found so many spies!"

"We will find just as many, perhaps," said Mrs. Strang, bitterly. "France is a republic and the United States is a republic. Does freedom breed traitors, I wonder?"

"I guess," Ruth said gently, "that we may have been too kind to certain classes of immigrants to the United States. Unused to liberty they spell it l-i-c-e-n-s-e."

"There are people other than ignorant foreigners who must be watched in these awful times," the matron said bitterly. "There are teachers in our colleges who sneer at patriotism just as they sneer at religion. Whisper, Miss Fielding! I am told that the very man they suspect in this dreadful thing—the American who has sold a map of this sector to the Germans—came from one of our foremost colleges, and is an American bred and born."

Ruth could not speak in answer to this. Her heart throbbed painfully in her throat. To so accuse Tom Cameron of heartless and dastardly treachery!

She could not defend him. To defend was to accuse! If everybody believed this awful thing—

Ruth was just as sure of Tom Cameron's guiltlessness as she was of her own faithfulness. But how damning the circumstantial evidence must be against him!

She was thankful she heard nothing more of this thing that night. Charlie and other men brought in the supplies. She could not arrange them then, for she was exhausted. She only waited to lock the door when all the supplies were placed, and then found the hut where the women of the Red Cross slept.

She had here a narrow cot, a locker and chair, and the privacy of a movable screen. Nothing else.

This was real "soldiering," as she soon found. Her experiences at Lyse and at Clair had been nothing like this. In one town she had lived at a pension, while at the latter hospital she had had her own little cell in the annex.

However, the girl of the Red Mill never thought of complaining. If these other earnest girls and women could stand such rough experiences why not she?

She slept and dreamed of home—of the Red Mill and Uncle Jabez and Aunt Alvirah Boggs, with her murmured, "Oh, my back! and oh, my bones!" She was again a child and roamed the woods and fields along the Lumano River with Tom Cameron and Helen.

"I wish I were at home! I wish I were at home!" was her waking thought.

It was the first time she had whispered that wish since leaving the States. But never before had her heart been so sore and her spirit so depressed.

When, some weeks before, she had believed Tom Cameron seriously wounded, she had been frightened and anxious only. Now the whole world seemed to have gone wrong. There was nobody with whom she could confer about this awful trouble.

She arose, and, after making her toilet and before breakfast, went out of the hut. She beheld an entirely different looking landscape from that which she was used to about Clair.

Through the gateway of the compound she saw a rutted road, with dun fields beyond. Behind, the ridge rose abruptly between the hospital and the battle front.

A red-headed young Irishman in khaki stood at the gateway, or tramped up and down with his rifle on his shoulder. He could not look at the girl without grinning, and Ruth smiled in return.

"'Tis a broth of a mornin', Miss," he whispered, as she drew near. "Be you the new lady Charlie Bra-a-agg brought over last night?"

"Yes. I am to take the place of the girl who—who——"

She faltered and could not go on. The Irish lad nodded and blinked rapidly.

"Bedad!" he muttered. "We'll make the Boches pay for that when we go over the top. Never fear."

He halted abruptly, became preternaturally grave, and presented arms. The young surgeon, Dr. Monteith, who had met Ruth the night before, tramped in from a morning walk.

"Good morning, Miss Fielding. Did you sleep?"

She confessed that she did. He smiled, but there was a deep crease between his eyes.

"I am glad you are up betimes. We need some of your supplies. Can I send the orderlies with the schedule soon?"

"Oh, yes! I will try to be ready in half an hour," she cried, turning quickly toward the hut, of which she carried the key.

"Wait! Wait!" he called. "No such hurry as all that. You have not breakfasted, I imagine? Well, never neglect your food. It is vital. I shall not send to you until half-past eight."

He saluted and went on. Ruth went to the hut in which the nurses messed. The night shift had just come in and she found them a pleasant, if serious, lot of women. And of all nationalities by blood—truly American!

There was an air about the nurses in the field hospital different from those she had met in institutions farther back from the battle line. There were serious girls there, but there was always a spatter of irresponsibles as well.

Here the nurses were like soldiers—and soldiers in active and dangerous service. There was a marked reserve about them and an expression of countenance that reminded Ruth of some of the nuns she had seen at home—a serenity that seemed to announce that they had given over worldly thoughts and that their minds were fixed upon higher things.

There was a hushed way of speaking, too, that impressed Ruth. It was as though they listened all the time for something. Was it for the whine of the shells that sometimes came over the ridge and dropped perilously near the hospital?

As the day went on, however, the girl found that there was considerably more cheerfulness and light-heartedness in and about the hospital than she supposed would be found here. Having straightened out her own hut and supplied the various wards with what they needed for the day, she went about, getting acquainted.

It was a large hospital and there were many huts. In each of these shelters were from two dozen to forty patients. A nurse and an orderly took care of each hut, with a night attendant. Everybody was busy.

There were many visitors, too—visitors of all kinds and for all imaginary reasons. People came in automobiles; these had passes from military authorities to see and bring comforts to the wounded. And there were more modest visitors who came on foot and brought baskets of jams and jellies and cakes and home-made luxuries that were eagerly welcomed by the wounded. For soldiers everywhere—whether well or ill—develop a sweet tooth.

Into the compound about midafternoon Ruth saw a tall figure slouch with a basket on his arm. It had begun to drizzle, as it so often does during the winter in Northern France, and this man wore a bedrabbled cloak—a brigandish-looking cloak—over his blue smock.

She had never seen such a figure before; and yet, there was something about the man that seemed familiar to the keen-eyed girl.

"Who is he?" she asked a nurse standing with her at the door of a ward, and pointing to the man slouching along with his basket across the open way.

"Oh, that? It is Nicko, the chocolate peddler," said the nurse carelessly. "A harmless fellow. Not quite right—here," and she tapped her own forehead significantly. "You understand? They say he lived here when first the Boches used their nasty gas, and he was caught in a cellar where a gas bomb exploded, and it affected his brain. It does that sometimes, you know," she added sadly.

Ruth's eyes had followed the chocolate seller intently. Around a corner of a hut swung the surgeon, who was already the girl's friend. He all but ran against the slouching figure, and he spoke sharply to the man.

For an instant the chocolate peddler straightened. He stood, indeed, in a very soldierly fashion. Then, as the quick-tempered surgeon strode on, Nicko bowed. He bowed from the hips—and Ruth gasped as she saw the obeisance. Only yesterday she had seen a man bow in that same way!

CHAPTER IX: COT 24—HUT H

The guns on the battle front had been silent for twenty-four hours; but there were whispers of the Yankees "getting back" at the Heinies in return for the outbreak of German gunfire which had startled Ruth Fielding the afternoon she had taken tea at the Chateau Marchand.

The outbreak of the new attack—this time from the American side—began about nine o'clock at night. A barrage was laid down, behind which, Ruth learned, several raiding parties would go over.

Just the method of this advance across No Man's Land Ruth did not understand. But all the time the guns were roaring back and forth (for, of course, the Germans quickly replied) she knew the American boys were in peril all along that sector.

That was a bad night for Ruth. She lay in her cot awake, but with her eyes closed, breathing deeply and regularly so that those about her thought she was asleep.

In the morning the matron said:

"You are really quite wonderful, Miss Fielding, to sleep through all that. I wish I could do the same."

And all night long Ruth had been praying—praying for the safety of the boys that had gone over the top, not for herself. That she was in danger did not greatly trouble her. She thought of the soldiers. She thought particularly of Tom Cameron—wherever he might be!

The flurry of gunfire was over by dawn. After breakfast Ruth went down to the gate. She had heard the ambulances rolling in for hours, and now she saw the stretcher-bearers stumbling into the receiving ward with the broken men. Here they were operated upon, when necessary, and sorted out—the grands blessés sent to the more difficult wards, the less seriously wounded to others.

Curiosity did not bring Ruth to the gate. It was in the hope of seeing Charlie Bragg that she went there. Nor was she disappointed.

His shaky old car rolled up with three men under the canvas and one with a bandaged arm sitting on the seat beside him. Charlie was pale and haggard. Half the top of the ambulance had been shot away since she had ridden in it, and the boy had roughly repaired the damage with a blanket. But he nodded to Ruth with his old cheerful grin. Nothing could entirely quench Charlie Bragg.

"Got tipped over and holed up in a marmite cave for a couple of hours during the worst of it last night," he told Ruth. "Never mind. It gave me another chapter for my new book. Surely! I'm going to write a second one. They all do, you know. You rather get the habit."

"But, Charlie! Is—is there any news?" she asked him, with shaking voice and eyes that told much of her anxiety.

He knew well what she meant, and he looked grim enough for a minute, and nodded.

"Yes. A little."

"Oh, Charlie! They—they haven't found him?"

"No. Maybe they'd better not," breathed the boy, shaking his head. "I don't think there's any hope, Miss Ruth."

"Oh, Charlie! He's not dead?"

"Better be," muttered the boy. "I wouldn't ask if I were you. It looks bad for him—everybody says so."

"You know him, Charlie Bragg!" she burst out angrily. "Can you believe Tom Cameron would do such a wicked thing as this they accuse him of?"

"We-ell. I don't want to believe it," he agreed. "But, look here!" and in desperation he pulled something from his pocket. "You know that, don't you?"

"Why! Tom's matchbox!" cried the girl, taking the silver box and seeing the initials of the lost soldier on the case. She had had it engraved herself—and Helen had paid for the box. They had given it to Tom when he went to Harvard for his Freshman course.

"Of course. I've seen him use it, too," Charlie Bragg hurried to say. "I knew it and begged it of the fellow who found it."

"Where did he find it?"

"You know, some of our boys went across and visited the Heinies last night," Charlie said gently. "They got right into the German trenches and drove out the Heinies. And in a German dugout—before they blew it up with bombs—this chap I talked with picked up that box."

"Oh, Charlie!" gasped the girl.

"Yes. He didn't see the significance of the monogram. He didn't know Mr. Cameron personally, I think. He was slightly wounded and I helped him with first aid. He gave the box to me as a German souvenir," and the driver of the ambulance looked grim.

"Then they surely have got poor Tom!" whispered Ruth.

"At least, it looks as though he went over that way," agreed the boy sadly.

"Don't speak so, Charlie!" she cried. "I tell you he has been taken prisoner."

"We-ell," drawled her friend again, "we can't know about that."

"But we will know!" she said, with added vehemence. "It will all come out in time. Only—it will be too late to help poor Tom, then."

"Gosh!" groaned Charlie Bragg. "It's too late to help him now—if you should ask me!"

Ruth had nobody to talk to about Tom Cameron save the young ambulance driver. And him she could see but seldom.

For fear of having to explain to her chum, she could not write to Helen Cameron, who was in Paris. Just now, too, she was too busy for letter writing.

Mrs. Strang found a girl to help Ruth in the supply hut, one who was willing and able to learn all about the merchandise under Ruth's care. The latter was not asked to remain at this hospital outpost for long. Her place was at Clair, and, until the Red Cross directors deliberately changed her, Ruth must give her first thought to the Clair Supply Headquarters.

She saw, however, that she would be several days at this field hospital. She had been glad to come in hope of learning something about Tom. Now she saw that she was doomed to disappointment.

This locality was the last place in which to search for news of the lost lieutenant. Everybody here (everybody who spoke of the matter at all) believed that Tom Cameron had played the traitor and, for money or some other unexplained reason, had gone over to the enemy.

"As though poor Tom could even dream of such a thing!" she thought.

She must keep her opinion to herself. She was too wise to start any argument on the affair. It might be, if she kept still, that she would learn something of significance that would lead to an explanation of the terrible event.

What she personally could do to save Tom's reputation she did not even imagine at the time. Nevertheless, there might be some chance of doing him a good turn.

As for his personal safety, she had lost all hope of that. She believed he had been captured by the Germans, and she had heard too many stories of their treatment of prisoners to hope that he would escape injury and actual torture.

It was said that the enemy would treat the first Americans captured with particular harshness, in hope of "frightening the Yankees." She knew that the advancing Canadians had found their captured brothers crucified on barn doors in the early months of the war. Why should the Yankees expect better treatment from the Huns?

With this load of anxiety and fear upon her heart, Ruth still found time for interest in what went on about her. She was an observant girl. And, as ever, her sympathies were touched in behalf of the wounded.

Although the American Red Cross had taken over this field hospital, most of the wounded were Frenchmen.

She was glad to see so many visitors daily bringing comforts for the men; but of all those who came she noted particularly the peculiar-looking Nicko, the chocolate vender. Daily he came, and Ruth always observed both his comings and goings.

Never did he fail to go into a particular ward—one of those in which the more seriously wounded patients lay—Hut H. She sometimes saw him going through the aisles at his funny, wabbling gait, offering his wares to the soldiers. The latter jeered at him, or joked with him, as their mood was. He wore an old battered hat, the brim of which flopped over his face and half masked his features.

One afternoon Ruth met the strange fellow at the door of Hut H. She was going out as he was coming in. The man backed away from her, mumbling. She threw a coin into his basket and took a small package of chocolate.

"Bien obligé, Mademoiselle!" he was startled into saying, and bowed to her. It was not the stiff, martial bow she had before noted, but the sweeping, ingratiating bow of the Frenchman. Ruth walked on, but she was startled.

Finally she turned swiftly and went back to the door of Hut H. The nurse on duty had just come from the end of the ward. Over her shoulder Ruth saw Nicko halt beside one of the cots far down the line.

"Who is that Nicko converses with?" Ruth asked idly.

"Oh, his friend, the Boche. Didn't you know we had a German officer with us? Cot 24. Not a bad fellow at all. Yes, Nicko never fails to sell our Boche friend chocolate. He is a regular customer."

"Cot 24—Hut H," Ruth repeated in her own mind. She would not forget that. And yet—did it mean anything? Was there something wrong with Nicko, the chocolate peddler?

CHAPTER X: DEVOURING SUSPICION

She had been at the field hospital for a week. It seemed to Ruth Fielding at last as though she could not remain "holed up" like a rabbit any longer.

At Clair she had been used to going out of the hospital when she liked and going anywhere she pleased. Here she found it was necessary to have a pass even to step out of the hospital compound.

"And be careful where you walk, Miss Fielding," said Dr. Monteith, as he signed her pass. "Do not go toward the battle front. If you do you may be halted."

"Halted!" repeated Ruth, not quite understanding.

"And perhaps suspected," he said, nodding gravely. "Even your Red Cross will not save you."

"Oh, dear me!" exclaimed the girl. "Is everybody suspected of spying? I think it has become a craze."

"We do not know whom to suspect," he said. "Our closest friends may be enemies. We cannot tell."

"But, Doctor Monteith, who are in this district save our soldiers and the French inhabitants?" asked Ruth.

"True. But there may be a traitor among us. Indeed, it is believed that there has been," and Ruth winced and looked away from him. "As for our allies here—well, all of them may not be above earning German gold. And they would think it was not as though they were betraying their own countrymen. There are only United States soldiers in this sector now, as you say, Miss Fielding."

"I cannot imagine people being so wicked," sighed the girl.

"No matter how it is done, or who does it, the enemy is getting information about our troops and condition, as the last two attacks have proved. So take care where you go, Miss Fielding, and what you do," he added earnestly.

She promised, and went away with her pass. It was late afternoon and her duties were over for the day. She would not be needed at the supply hut until morning. And, indeed, the girl she was breaking in was already mastering the details of the work. Ruth could soon go back to her own work at Clair.

She walked nimbly out of the compound gate, making sure that she was following a road that led away from the front. Nobody halted her. Indeed, she was soon passing through a little valley that seemed as peaceful and quiet as though there was no such thing as war in the world.

The path she followed was plainly but a farm track. It wound between narrow fields that had not been plowed the season before—not even by cannon-shot. Somehow the big shells had flown over this little valley.

The sun was setting, and the strip of western sky above the hills was tinged with his golden glories. Already pale twilight lay in the valley. But in this latitude the twilight would long remain. She did not hasten her steps, nor did she soon turn back toward the field hospital.

She saw a cottage half hidden behind a hedge of evergreens. It stood in a small square of muddy garden. There was a figure at work in this patch—the tall, stoop-shouldered figure of a man. He was digging parsnips that had been left out for the frost to sweeten.

He used the mattock slowly and methodically. With the cottage as a background, and the muddy bit of garden, the picture he made was typical of the country and the people who inhabited it.

Suddenly she realized that she recognized the ragged blue smock and the old droop-brimmed hat he wore. It was Nicko, the chocolate vender. This must be his place of abode.

Ruth hesitated. She had felt some shrinking from the man before; now she realized she was afraid of him. He had not seen her and she stood back and watched him.

Of a sudden another man appeared from around the corner of the cottage. Ruth was more than glad, then, that she had not shown herself. She turned to retrace her steps.

Then she looked again at this new figure in the picture. She almost spoke aloud in her amazement. The newcomer was dressed exactly as Nicko was dressed—the same blue and ragged smock, shapeless trousers, wooden shoes, and with a hat the twin of the one the first Nicko wore. Indeed, it was a second Nicko who stood there in the bit of garden before the laborer's cot.

But amazement and suspicion did not hold her to the spot for long. She did not wish to be discovered by the pair. She was confident now that there was something altogether wrong with Nicko the chocolate peddler—and his double!

Out of view of the cottage she hurried her steps. Through the gloaming she sped up the path in the valley toward the high-road on which faced the hospital stockade.

Her thoughts were in a tangle of doubt. Yet one clear thread of determination she held. She must give her confidence to somebody—she must relate her suspicions to some person who was in authority.

Not the medical chief of staff at this field hospital. Nor did she wish to go to the commanding officer of this sector, whoever he might be. Indeed, she almost feared to talk with any American officer, for Tom Cameron seemed to be entangled in this web of deceit and treachery into which she believed she had gained a look.

There was a man whom she could trust, however; one who would know exactly what to do, she felt sure. And it would be his business to examine into the mystery. The moment she returned to Clair Ruth would get into communication with this individual.

Thus thinking, she hurried on and had almost reached the highway when something made her look back. Not a sound; for even the sleepy birds had stopped twittering and there was no rustle of night wind in the bare shrubbery about her.

But mysteriously she was forced to turn her head. She looked down the path over which her feet had sped from the laborer's cot. There was something behind her!

Ruth did not scream. A form came up the track swiftly and at first she saw it so indistinctly that she had no idea what it really was. Had she been spied by the men in the garden, and was one of them following her?

She trembled so that she could not walk. She crouched back against the hedge, watching fearfully the on-rush of the phantom-like apparition coming so swiftly up the path.

CHAPTER XI: THE FLYING MAN

While yet the silent figure was some rods away Ruth Fielding realized that it was no human being. It was not one of the men she had seen in the garden of Nicko's cottage.

This creature came too swiftly up the path and skimmed the ground too closely. A light-colored object—swift, silent and threatening of aspect.

The girl shrank against the hedge, and the next instant—with a rush of passage that stirred the air all about her—the Thing was gone! It was again that strange and incomprehensible apparition of the werwolf!

If it was Bubu, the greyhound she had seen at the Chateau Marchand, he was much lighter in color than when he appeared pacing beside his mistress on the chateau lawns. The phantom had dashed past so rapidly that, in the gathering dusk, Ruth could make out little of its real appearance.

Headed toward the battle lines, it had disappeared within seconds. The girl, her limbs still trembling, followed in haste to the highway. Already the creature had been swallowed up in the shadows.

She went on toward the hospital gateway and had scarcely recovered her self-control when she arrived there. Altogether, her evening's experience had been most disconcerting.

The two men, dressed alike and apparently of the same height and shambling manner, whom she had seen in Nicko's garden, worried her quite as much—indeed, worried her even more than the sight of the mysterious creature the peasants called the werwolf.

More than ever was she determined to take into her confidence somebody who would be able to explain the mystery of it all. At least, he would be able to judge if what made her so anxious was of moment.

And Tom Cameron's disappearance, too! Ruth's worry of mind regarding her old friend propped her eyes open that night.

In the morning she went over the stock shelves again with the girl she had trained, and finally announced to Mrs. Strang that she felt she must return to Clair. After all, she had been assigned to the job there and must not desert it.

An ambulance was going down to Clair with its burden of wounded men, and Ruth was assigned to the seat beside the driver. He chanced to be "Cub" Holdness, one of the ambulance drivers to whom Ruth had been introduced by Charlie Bragg at Mother Gervaise's cottage the night of her trip up to the field hospital.

Holdness was plainly delighted to have the girl with him for the drive to Clair. He was a Philadelphia boy, and he confessed to having had no chance to drive a girl—even in an ambulance—since coming over.

"I had one of those 'reckless roadsters' back home," he sighed. "Dad said every time his telephone rang he expected it was me calling from some outlying police station for him to come and bail me out for overspeeding.

"And there was a bunch of girls I knew who were just crazy to have me take 'em for a spin out around Fairmount Park and along the speedways. Just think, Miss Fielding, of the difference between those times and these," and he nodded solemnly.

"I should say there was a difference," laughed Ruth, trying to appear in good spirits. "Don't you get dreadfully tired of all these awful sights and sounds?"

"No. Excitement keeps us keyed up, I guess," he replied. "You know, there is almost always something doing."

"I should say there was!"

She saw that while he talked he did not for a moment forget that he was driving three sorely wounded men. He eased the ambulance over the rough parts of the road and around the sharp turns with infinite skill. It was actually wonderful how smoothly the ambulance ran.

Occasionally they were caught in a tight corner and the machine jounced so that moans of agony were wrung from the lips of the wounded behind them on the stretchers. This, however, occurred but seldom.

Once one of the men begged for water—water to drink and its coolness on his head. They were passing a trickling stream that looked clear and refreshing.

"Let me get out a moment and get him some," begged Ruth.

"Can't do it. Against orders. We're commanded not to taste water from any stream, spring, or well in this sector—let alone give it to the wounded. Nobody knows when the water is poisoned."

"But the Germans have been gone from this district so long now!" she cried.

"They may have their spies here. In fact," grumbled Holdness, "we are sure they do have friends in the sector."

"Oh!"

"You know that Devil Corner Charlie Bragg drove you past the other night? The shells have torn that all to pieces. We have to go fully two miles around by another road to get to Clair. We don't pass Mother Gervaise's place any more."

Ruth looked at him sadly but questioningly.

"Do you believe that story they tell about one of our young officers having gone over to the enemy?" she asked.

Holdness flushed vividly. "I didn't know him. I've got no opinion on the matter, Miss Fielding," he said. "But somebody has mapped out the whole sector for the Huns—and it has cost lives, and ammunition. You can't blame folks for being suspicious."

The answer quenched her conversation. Ruth scarcely spoke again during the remainder of the journey.

They welcomed her in most friendly fashion at the Clair Hospital. But the first thing she did after depositing her bag in her cell was to go to the telegraph office and put before the military censor the following message addressed to the prefect of police at Lyse,

"Will you please communicate with M. Lafrane. I have something of importance to tell him."

She signed her name and occupation in full to this, and was finally assured that it would be sent. M. Lafrane was of the secret police, and Ruth Fielding had been in communication with him on a previous occasion.

Several days passed with no reply from her communication to the police. Nor did any news reach her from the field hospital where she had been engaged, nor from her friends at the front. Indeed, those working near the battle lines really know less of what is being done in this war than civilians in America, for instance.

Almost every night the guns thundered, and it was reported that the Americans were making sorties into the German lines and bearing back both prisoners and plunder. But just what was being accomplished Ruth Fielding had no means of knowing.

Not having seen or heard from Henriette Dupay since her return, early in the following week Ruth started out to walk briskly to the Dupay farm one afternoon.

Of late the aeroplanes had become very numerous over this sector. They were, for the most part, American machines. But this afternoon she chanced to see one of the French Nieuports at close quarters.

These are the scouting, or battle planes, and carry but two men and a machine gun. She heard the motor some moments before seeing the aeroplane rise over the tree tops. She knew it must have leaped from a large field on this side of the Dupay farm and not far below the gateway of the Chateau Marchand.

Ruth stopped to gaze upward at the soaring airplane. Her figure stood out plainly in the country road and the two men aboard the Nieuport must have immediately spied her.

The machine dipped and scaled downward until she could have thrown a stone upward and hit it. One of the men—masked and helmeted as the flying men always are—leaned from his seat, and she saw him looking down upon her through the tangle of stay-wires.

Then he dropped a small white object that fell like a plummet at her feet!

"What in the world can that be?" murmured the girl to herself.

For a breath she was frightened. Although the aeroplane carried the French insignia it might be an enemy machine. She, too, was obsessed with the fear of spies!

But the object that fell was not an explosive bomb. It was a weighted ball of oiled silk. As the machine soared again and rapidly rose to the upper air levels, the girl picked up the strange object and burst it open.

The lead pellets that weighted the globe were scattered on the ground. Within there was nothing else but a strip of heavy document paper. On this was traced in a handwriting she knew well, this unsigned message:

"Don't believe everything you hear."

It was Tom Cameron's handwriting—and Ruth knew that the message was meant for her eye and her eye only!

CHAPTER XII: AUNT ABELARD

Of course nothing just like this ever happened save in a fairy story—or in real life. The paper without address, but meant only for Ruth Fielding, had fallen from the aeroplane. She had seen it fall at her feet and could not be mistaken.

Who the two men in the French Nieuport were she could not know. Masked and hooded as they were, she could distinguish the features of neither the pilot nor the man who had dropped the paper bomb. But—she was sure of this—they were somehow in communication with Tom Cameron.

And Tom Cameron was supposed to have gone across the lines to the Germans, or—as Ruth believed—had been captured by them. Yet, if he was a captive, how had he been able to send her this message?

Again, how did he know she was worried about him? He must have reason to suspect that a story was being circulated regarding his unfaithfulness.

Who were those two flying men? Were they German spies? Had Tom been a prisoner in the hands of the Huns, would spies have brought this word from him to her?

And how—and how—and how——?

Her queries and surmises were utterly unanswerable. She turned the bit of paper over and over in her fingers. She could not be mistaken about Tom's handwriting. He had penciled those words.

It was true, any friend of Tom's who knew his handwriting and might have picked up the loaded paper bomb, would have considered the written line a personal message.

"Don't believe everything you hear."

But, then, what friends had Tom in this sector of the battle front save his military associates and Ruth Fielding? The girl never for one moment considered that the written line might have been meant for anybody but herself.

And she did with it the very wisest thing she could have done. She tore the paper into the tiniest of bits, and, as she continued her walk to the Dupay farm, she dribbled the scraps along the grassy road.

She began to have a faint and misty idea of what it all meant—Tom's disappearance, the general belief among his comrades that he was a traitor, and this communication which had reached her hands in seemingly so wonderful a manner.

Tom Cameron had been selected for some dangerous and secret mission. It might have occasioned his entrance through the enemy's lines. He was on secret service beyond the great bombarding German guns!

If this was so he was in extreme peril! But he was doing his duty!

Ruth's heart throbbed to the thought—to both thoughts! His dangerous work was not done yet. But it was very evident that he had means of knowing what went on upon this side of the line of battle.

The men recently flying over her head in the French air machine must be comrades of Tom's in the secret mission which had carried that young fellow into the enemy's country. The message she had received might be only one of several the flying men had dropped about Clair, and at the request of Tom Cameron, the latter hoping that at least one of them would reach Ruth's hands.

The girl knew that American and French flying men often carried communications addressed to the German people into Germany, and dropped them in similar "bombs." One of the President's addresses had been circulated through a part of Germany and Austria by this means.

She had a feeling, too, that the man who had thrown the message to her knew her. But Ruth could not imagine who he was. She might have believed it to be Tom Cameron himself; only she knew very well that Tom had not joined the air service.

The incident, however, heartened her. Whatever Tom was doing—no matter how perilous his situation—he had thought of her. She had an idea that the message had been written within a few hours.

She went on more cheerfully toward the Dupay farm. She arrived amidst a clamor of children and fowls, to find the adult members of the family gathered in the big living-room of the farmhouse instead of occupied, as usual, about the indoor and outdoor work. For the Dupays were no sluggards.

"Oh, Mademoiselle Ruth!" cried Henriette, and ran to meet her. The French girl's plump cheeks were tear-streaked and Ruth instantly saw that not only the girl but the whole family was much disturbed.

"What has happened?" the American girl asked.

In these days of war almost any imaginable thing might happen.

"It is poor old Aunt Abelard!" Henriette exclaimed in her own tongue. "She must remove from her old home at Nacon."

Ruth knew that the place was a little village (and villages can be small, indeed, in France) between Clair and the field hospital where she had herself been for a week, but on another road than that by which she had traveled.

"It is too near the battle line," she said to Henriette. "Don't you think she should have moved long ago?"

"But the Germans left it intact," Henriette declared. "She is very comfortable there. She does not wish to leave. Oh, Mademoiselle Ruth! could you not speak to some of your gr-r-reat, gr-r-reat, brave American officers and have it stopped?"

"Have what stopped?" cried Ruth in amazement.

"Aunt Abelard's removal."

"Are the Americans making her leave her home?"

"It is so!" Henriette declared.

"It is undoubtedly necessary then," returned Ruth gently.

"It is not understood. If she could remain there throughout the German invasion, and was undisturbed by our own army, why should these Americans plague her?"

Henriette spoke with some heat, and Ruth saw that her mother and the grandmother were listening. Their faces did not express their usual cheerful welcome with which Ruth had become familiar. Aunt Abelard's trouble made a difference in their feeling toward the Americans, that was plain.

Nor was this to be wondered at. The French farmer is as deeply rooted in his soil as the great trees of the French forests. That is why their treatment by the German invader and the ruin of their farms have been so great a cross for them to shoulder.

Ruth learned that Aunt Abelard—an aunt of Farmer Dupay, and a widow—had lived upon her little place since her marriage over half a century before. Without her little garden and her small fields, and her cow and pig and chickens, she would scarcely know how to live. And to be uprooted and carried to some other place! It was unthinkable!

"It is fierce!" said Henriette in good American, having learned that much from Charlie Bragg.

"I am sure there must be good reason for it," Ruth said. "I will inquire. If there is any possibility of her remaining without being in danger——"

"What danger?" demanded Madame Dupay, clicking her tongue. "Do these countrymen of yours intend to let the Boches overrun our country again? Our poilus drove them back and kept them back."

Ruth saw she could say nothing to appease the rising wrath of the family. She was rather sorry she had chanced to come upon this day of ill-tidings.

"Of course she will come here?" she asked Henriette.

"Where else can she go?"

"Will your father go after her in the automobile?"

"What?" gasped Henriette. "That is of the devil's concoction, so thinks poor Aunt Abelard. She will not ride in it. And my father is busy. Let the Yankees bring her—and her goods—if they desire to remove her from her own abode."

Ruth could say nothing to soothe either her little friend nor the other members of the family. They could not understand why Aunt Abelard must be removed from her place; nor did Ruth understand.

She was convinced, however, that there must be something of importance afoot in this sector, and that Aunt Abelard's removal from her little cottage was a necessity. The American troops in France were not deliberately making enemies among the farming people.

Henriette walked for some distance toward the hospital when Ruth went back; but the French girl was gloomy and had little to say to her American friend.

When Ruth reached the hospital and was ascending to her cell at the back, the matron came hurrying through the corridor to meet her. She was plainly excited.

"Mademoiselle Fielding!" she cried. "You have a visitor. In the office. Go to him at once, my dear. It is Monsieur Lafrane."

CHAPTER XIII: AN UNEXPECTED MEETING

Monsieur Lafrane Ruth could count as one of her friends. Not many months before she had enabled the secret service man to solve a criminal problem and arrest several of the criminals engaged in a conspiracy against the Red Cross.

She had not been sure that he would so quickly respond to her telegram to the elderly prefect of police at Lyse, who was likewise her friend and respectful admirer.

This secret agent was a lean man of dark complexion. His manner was cordial when he rose to greet her. She knew that he was a very busy man and that he had responded personally to her appeal because he took a deeper interest in her than in most people aside from those whose acts it was his duty to investigate.

They were alone in the small office of the hospital. He said crisply and in excellent English: "Mademoiselle has need of me?"

"I have something to tell you, Monsieur—something that I think may be of importance. Yet, as we Americans say, I may be merely stirring up a mare's nest."

"Ah, I understand the reference," he said, smiling. "Let me be the judge of the value of what you tell me, Mademoiselle. Proceed."

Swiftly she told him of her visit to the field hospital so much nearer the battle line than this quiet institution at Clair, and, in addition, told him of Nicko, the chocolate peddler, and his dual appearance.

"There are two of the men. They dress exactly alike. I was suspicious of the peddler the very first time I saw him. No Frenchman—not even a French soldier—bows as I saw him bow."

"Ha!" ejaculated the secret agent.

"He bows from the hips—the bow of a German military man. I—I have seen them bow before," Ruth hesitated, remembering Major Henri Marchand. "You understand?"

"But, yes, Mademoiselle," said the Frenchman, his eyes flashing.

"Then," she went on, "I saw the man—or supposedly the same man—a second time. He bowed very differently—just as an ordinary humble French peasant might bow."

"Could it not be that he forgot the second time you saw him?" queried M. Lafrane.

"I doubt it. There is something quite distinct in the air of the two men. But I understand that whichever comes to the hospital with the basket of sweets always has a word with the German officer in Hut H, Cot Twenty-four. You can easily find out about him."

"True," murmured the secret agent eagerly.

Then she told him of her walk in the gloaming and what she had seen in the garden of the peasant's cot—the two men dressed exactly alike. One must be the half-foolish Nicko; the other must be the spy.

M. Lafrane nodded eagerly again, pursing his lips.

"Mademoiselle," he said quietly, "I will ask the good madame if you may be relieved for the day. I have a car outside—a swift car. Can you show me that cottage—Nicko's dwelling? I will bring you back immediately."

"Of a surety," she told him in his own tongue, as he had spoken. "Wait. I will get my hat and coat. I may not know the nearest way to the place. But——"

"I am familiar with this territory," he said dryly. "We can strike it, I have no doubt, Mademoiselle. But I need you to verify the place and—perhaps—to identify the man."

"Not the spy?" she gasped.

"Nicko, the peddler."

"I see. I will be with you in the courtyard at once, Monsieur."

When she came out he was ready to step into a two-seated roadster, hung low and painted a battleship gray. A man in uniform on the front seat drove. Ruth got in, was followed by the secret agent, and they started.

She had much more in her heart and mind; but she doubted the advisability of telling M. Lafrane.

There was what she suspected about Major Henri Marchand. Could she turn suspicion toward the son of her good friend, the countess? And his brother who, it was said, had run away?

Ruth felt that she had already told much that might cause the major trouble. She did not know. She only suspected.

As for Tom Cameron's trouble—and the mystery surrounding him—she did not feel that she could speak to the secret agent about that. Tom's affairs could have nothing to do with the work of this French criminal investigator. No. She hugged to her heart all her anxiety regarding Tom.

As soon as they left the hospital courtyard Ruth found that she was traveling with a chauffeur beside whom Charlie Bragg's reckless driving was tame indeed. Besides, Charlie's lame car could not arrive at such speed as this racing type of automobile was capable of.

By looking over the back of the front seat she obtained a glimpse of the speedometer, and saw the indicator traveling from sixty to seventy. After that she did not wish to look again. She did not want to know if they traveled faster.

The road over which they went was strange to Ruth Fielding. It was by a much shorter way Charlie Bragg had taken her to the field hospital, and over which she had returned.

They began before long to meet farmers' wagons, piled high with household goods, on which sat the strange, sad-eyed children of the war zone, or decrepit old people, often surrounded by their fowls. For even the poorest and most destitute of the French peasants manage to have "poulets."

The processions of moving people amazed Ruth. She remembered what the Dupays had said about Aunt Abelard, and she began to see that there was a general exodus being forced from the country nearer the front in this sector.

It was a fact that the people did not look happy. Now and then one of the American military police walked beside a wagon, as though he had been sent on with the movers to make sure that they kept moving.

The girl asked M. Lafrane nothing about this exodus. Perhaps he knew no more the reason for it than Ruth did.

They came to a little dale between hills at last, and in this place stood a cottage and barns—a tiny homestead, but very neat, and one that had been unmarred by the enemy. There were even fruit trees standing.

There was a huge wagon before the door, and into it must go the household goods and the family as well—if there was a family. It seemed that the wagon had just arrived, and the American soldiers with it scarcely knew what to do in this case. There was nothing packed, ready for removal, and an old woman—the only person about the farmstead—was busy feeding her flock of chickens.

"You must come, vite, Tante," Ruth heard the corporal in charge of the squad say to the old woman. The automobile had stopped, for the road was too narrow for it to pass the wagon.

The old woman seemed to understand the American's mixture of English and French. She shook her head with emphasis.

"But I cannot leave my pullets," she said, aghast. "They will starve. You will go along, you Americans, and leave me alone."

"You must come, Tante," repeated the corporal, inflexibly. "You should have prepared for this. You were warned in time." Then to his men: "Go in, boys, and bring out her goods. Careful, now. Don't mess anything up."

"You cannot take my things. Your cart is already full," shrilled the old woman. "And my pullets!"

The American soldiers entered the cottage. Between her anger at them and her fear for the safety of her chickens, the old woman was in a pitiful state, indeed. Ruth looked at M. Lafrane.

"Oh, can we not do anything for her?" she asked.

"Military law knows no change—the laws of the Medes and Persians," he said grimly. "She must go, of course——"

Suddenly he sat up more stiffly beside the American girl and his hand went to his cap in salute. He even rose, and, before Ruth looked around and spied the occasion for this, she knew it must foretell the approach of an officer of importance.

Coming along the road (he had been sheltered from her gaze before by the laden wagon) was a French officer in a very brilliant uniform. Ruth gasped aloud; she knew him at a glance.

It was Major Henri Marchand, in the full panoply of a dress uniform, although he was on foot. He acknowledged M. Lafrane's salute carelessly and did not see the girl at all. He walked directly into the yard surrounding the cottage. The corporal of the American squad was saying:

"I am sorry for you, ma mère. But we cannot wait now. You should have been ready for us. You have had forty-eight hours' notice."

The old countrywoman was quite enraged. She began to vilify the Americans most abominably. Ruth suddenly heard her say that the Abelards had been rooted here for generations. She refused to go for all the soldiers in the world!

Then she shrieked again as she saw the men bringing out her best bed. Major Marchand took a hand in the matter.

"Tante," he said quietly, "I am sorry for you. But these men are in the right. The high authorities have said you must go. All your neighbors are going. It is for la patrie. These are bitter times and we must all make sacrifices. Come, now, you must depart."

Ruth wondered at his quiet, yet forceful, manner. The corporal stood back, thankful to have the disagreeable duty taken out of his hands. And the American girl wondered, too, at the respect Monsieur Lafrane had shown this French officer. Had he saluted the uniform, or was Major Marchand a very important personage? Her brain was in a whirl of doubt.

CHAPTER XIV: MORE SACRIFICES THAN ONE

Monsieur Lafrane had stepped out of the automobile, although the wagon had now been backed so that the car could have easily passed. Its engine was still throbbing.

Ruth Fielding was giving her full attention to the little scene at the hencoop.

The tall, handsome major in his beautiful uniform made little impression upon the old woman. She backed away from him, pressing closer to the lathe coop.

"No, no! I will not come. My pullets—they will starve," she reiterated endlessly.

"But the Germans may be coming," the major said patiently. "They will kill your pullets and eat them."

"They did not do so before when they came," she shrieked. "I do not believe they are coming. These wicked Americans want my pullets. That is what it is! I will not!"

"Tante——" the major interposed gently.

"I will not, I tell you!" she interrupted.

She had backed up against the gate of the coop and had been fiddling behind her at its fastenings. Now, quick as a wink, she snatched the gate open and, with wonderful celerity for one of her age, plunged into the hencoop and slammed to the door.

There was a tumultuous flapping and cackling of the bewildered poultry, and the air inside the coop was immediately filled with dust and feathers. Then the chaos subsided and the old woman looked out defiantly at the major and at the half-amused, half-pitying soldier boys.

The major's shrug was characteristic. He turned to look at the spectators, and Ruth saw that his eyes were moist. His pity for the unfortunate old woman and his kindness to her had its effect upon the American girl. She wondered what manner of man, after all, this Frenchman could be.

Major Marchand said something in a low voice to the American corporal. The latter gave an order to his men. They surrounded the coop, and suddenly, at the word, the corners were torn apart and the walls of the enclosure thrown down.

Aunt Abelard shrieked—and so did the pullets. Many of the latter were caught on the wing by the soldiers. The major put his arm about the old woman's shoulders. She was shrieking insanely, but he led her into the house and there remained while most of the pullets were decapitated swiftly and thrown aside, to be later carried to the field kitchens.

But when the tearful old woman was brought out with the last of her possessions and bundled into the rear of the now loaded wagon, the American corporal came with a pair of the nicest pullets, their legs tied together, and placed them in the old woman's lap along with the bird-cage one of the boys lifted up to her.

Ruth, watching closely, saw Major Marchand draw the corporal aside and place a couple of twenty-franc notes in his hand, nodding toward the old woman. It was to recompense her for the pullets, over whose untimely fate she was still moaning.

The mystery of the major—or his character and what and who he really was—disturbed Ruth. She was excited. Should she tell Monsieur Lafrane of her suspicion that this officer of the French army was the man whom she thought was Nicko's double?

For it was Major Henri Marchand Ruth believed she had seen enter Nicko's garden and talk with him the evening before she left the field hospital to return to Clair.

The major walked quietly away without even seeing Ruth. The chauffeur of their car, after a nod from Lafrane, started again. They passed the wagon, which was already trundling down the road.

This cot was the last one at which Ruth saw anybody during that ride. For when they reached the hut of Nicko, the chocolate peddler, his place was likewise deserted. There were no neighboring houses.

Lafrane got out at Nicko's cottage and searched the premises. His face was grave when he came back to the car and told the chauffeur to hurry on to the hospital.

Here Ruth was amazed to see many American soldiers at work. They were piling sandbags about the various huts and over their roofs. She understood now why the people were being entirely cleared out of this sector. A great bombardment was expected.

Ruth did not get out of the car. M. Lafrane ran in, and, through the open gateway, she saw that he entered Hut H. He had gone to take a look at the occupant of Cot 24—the German officer.

He was occupied within some time and when he appeared at the door of the hut Dr. Monteith was with him. The two stood talking for a while before the secret agent returned to the gate. He got into the car again with just a word to his chauffeur.

"Mademoiselle," said M. Lafrane, his face serious, indeed, "there are many disappointments in life, as well as many sacrifices. We saw the old woman torn from her home—and from her pullets—just now. The pattern of life is complex for us all."

"I have come from Paris because you called me." Ruth started and looked at him closely. "I hoped that you might have something of moment to tell me. I shall always trust in your good sense."

Ruth felt a sinking of the heart.

"But, Monsieur! have I brought you here for nothing? I warned you it might be a mare's nest."

"Non, non!" he replied eagerly. "It is not your fault. I believe you did hand me a thread of a clue that might—under more fortunate circumstances—have led to the disclosure of something momentous."

"But that in reality leads nowhere, Monsieur. Is that what you mean?"

"Mademoiselle, Fate tricks us! This Nicko is one of those thrust out of this sector in haste because of military reasons. And the German Hauptman, who lay so long ill in that Hut H—well, Mademoiselle, he has died!"

Ruth was amazed, and for a time dumb. Should she bring Major Henri Marchand into the matter? The secret agent knew him and respected him. Ruth shrank from putting suspicion upon a possibly innocent person.

And yet, his height, his manner of bowing, an indefinite air about him, had convinced Ruth that Nicko's double was Henri Marchand. Who else could it be? Could there be some person who so resembled the countess' younger son?

The thought roweled her mind. There was something in it to be considered. Who else could the mysterious man be?

And then, of a sudden, it flashed into Ruth's mind. The older son of the Countess Marchand was probably in appearance like his brother. Count Allaire Marchand! And where was Count Allaire now?

The story was that the young count had disappeared from Paris. He was believed to be in the pay of the Germans. He, like Henri, had been educated in the Prussian military schools. No matter what the secret agents thought of the countess the loyalty of her sons was questioned by the peasants living about the chateau.

A determination grew in Ruth Fielding's mind. She would go to the chateau and see if there was a picture of Count Allaire in his old home. She wished to determine if he looked like Major Henri Marchand.

Meanwhile they rode swiftly over another road toward Clair. It was the road beside which the little inn of Mother Gervaise was situated.

Even that had been stripped of the widow's possessions and she was gone. Like every other cot in all this sector, and back for ten miles from the battle front, the place was deserted.

CHAPTER XV: BUBU

Ruth arrived at Clair again late in the evening and bade Monsieur Lafrane good-night at the hospital entrance. On the following day the girl of the Red Mill was permitted to go to the Chateau Marchand to call.

The secret agent had made it plain to Ruth that he held her in no fault for the seeming fiasco of their journey to the field hospital and its vicinity. The sudden death of the German officer in Hut H had been an act beyond human control. The disappearance of Nicko, the chocolate peddler, was an act of the military authorities.

On her own part Ruth was so confused regarding Major Henri Marchand that she dared not mention his name to Monsieur Lafrane. Matters must take their natural course—for a time, at least.

Nevertheless, the American girl had a particular object in mind when she set forth briskly for the chateau on this afternoon. She was free until bedtime, and during this contemplated call on the countess she was determined to learn what the young Count Marchand looked like.

On the edge of the town she spied an automobile approaching, and soon recognized Henriette Dupay behind the windshield. Ruth stopped and waved her hand. For a moment she thought the French girl was disinclined to stop at all.

However, Ruth did not propose to give Henriette an opportunity to show any unfriendliness. She liked the girl and she understood that the whole matter would be smoothed over in time. The reason for Aunt Abelard's uprooting would become apparent to the French people, and their momentary feeling against the Americans would change.

Henriette's face was quite flushed, however, when she stopped her car and returned briefly Ruth's greeting.

"How is Aunt Abelard?" the latter asked. She told Henriette how she had chanced to be present when the old woman was forced to leave her homestead.

"Ah, Mademoiselle, she is heart-broken!" declared Henriette, quite eschewing English now. "Yes, heart-broken! She arrived at our house with only two pullets. All the others were stolen by the Americans," and the girl tossed her head angrily.

"How about the forty francs she was given in lieu of the pullets?" Ruth asked, laughing. "Did she tell you about that?"

"But yes," returned the French girl, rather taken aback. "But that was given to her by Major Henri Marchand. He is so good!"

"True. But it is probable that she will make application to the American officers and will be reimbursed a second time," Ruth said dryly. "As far as the pullets go, Henriette, I believe they are a small loss to Aunt Abelard."

"But her house! Her home!" ejaculated the French girl.

"Of what use would that be to her had she remained and there should come the bombardment that everybody says is coming? The German shells may tear her cottage to bits."

Henriette shrugged her truly French shoulders. She evidently did not believe in the threatened bombardment. The guns of the front had been quiet for two days.

So she nodded to Ruth rather coldly and drove on into town. But Ruth went away smiling. She was quite convinced that Henriette and her family would soon find out their mistake, and then they would be on friendly terms with her again. The Latin nature is easily offended; but it is usually just.

She saw nobody else in her walk to the chateau. There she had to wait for some minutes at the gate for Dolge to answer her summons.

"The Mademoiselle Fielding," he said, bowing. "I am sure the countess will approve my asking you in at once. She is fond of you, Mademoiselle."

"I am glad, Dolge. I like to have people approve of me," smiled Ruth.

"Ah, yes, Mademoiselle. And the major—our Henri, our cadet! I am sure he approves of you, Mademoiselle."

The American girl flushed warmly, but managed to hide her disturbed countenance from the old serving man.

"He is not at home, is he, Dolge?" she quietly asked.

"But, no, Mademoiselle. He went hurriedly yesterday. And would you believe it?"

"Believe what?"

"He went in one of those flying machines. Oui! Oui! Right up into the sky, Mademoiselle," went on the old man excitedly. "Yonder he mounted it beyond the gates. Ah, these times! It is so that soon one will take an aeroplane as one takes a taxicab in the city. Is it not?"

Ruth listened and marveled. Major Marchand flying into the air from the chateau here on yesterday, when it was only yesterday that she met him, in his brave uniform, taking pity on a poor old woman who was driven out of the battle zone?

Suddenly her mind caught the point. The cogs slipped into juxtaposition, as it were, and everything unrolled in its proper sequence before her.

It was on yesterday, as she went toward the Dupay farm, that she had seen the rising aeroplane, from which had been dropped the paper bomb, wherein Ruth had found the message from Tom Cameron. It was from just beyond the gates that Dolge said the machine rose that had borne away Major Marchand from the chateau.

"The time, Dolge?" she demanded, stopping short in the walk and looking at the surprised old servant. "The time that Major Henri flew away?"

"Oh, la! It was around one of the clock. Not later."

That was the hour! Ruth was confident she was making no mistake now. It was either the major, or the pilot of the plane, that had dropped the message to her. Two hours and a half later she had seen the major at the cot of Aunt Abelard. He might easily have flown clear beyond the German lines and back again by that time. And he might easily have worn his major's uniform beneath his other garments.

But Tom's message. That was the point that puzzled her. If dropped by Major Marchand, how had he obtained it? What did the French officer, whose loyalty she doubted, have to do with Tom Cameron, whose loyalty she never for a moment doubted?

Ruth went on ahead of the wondering Dolge, vastly troubled. At every turn she was meeting incidents or surprising discoveries that entangled her mind more and more deeply in a web of doubt and mystery.

Where was Tom? Where did the major fly to? Where was he coming from when she had seen him walking down that country road where Aunt Abelard was having her unfortunate argument with the American soldiers?

The twists and turns of this mystery were enough to drive the girl distracted. And each incident which rose seemed to be dovetailed to some other part of the mystery.

Now she was suddenly sorry that she had not opened her heart entirely to Monsieur Lafrane. She wished she had told him about Tom Cameron, and the fears she felt for him, and what was said about him by his comrades. He might at least have been able to advise her.

She came to the chateau, therefore, in a most uncertain frame of mind. She was really in no mood for a social call.

But there was the countess walking on the paved court before the main door of the chateau. It was a fine day, and she walked up and down, with a shawl about her shoulders, humming a cheerful little song.

"Dear Mademoiselle Ruth!" she said, giving the girl her hands—soft and white, with a network of blue veins on their backs. "I am charmed. If it were not for you and our little Hetty I should scarcely feel I had a social life at all."

She spoke to Dolge as he hobbled away.

"Tell them to make tea," she said.

"Yes, Madame la Countess," he mumbled.

She took the arm of the strong young girl and walked with her up and down the portico.

"Henri will be disappointed in not seeing you, Mademoiselle. He went yesterday—called back to his duties."

"And by aeroplane, they tell me," answered the girl.

"Think!" exclaimed the countess, shrugging her shoulders. "A few months ago the thought of one of my boys mounting into the air would have kept me awake all of the night. And I slept like a child!"

"We grow used to almost everything, do we not?" Ruth said.

"War changes our outlook on life. Of course, I am not assured that he safely landed yesterday——"

"I can assure you of that, Madame, myself," said Ruth, without thinking far ahead when she said it.

"You, Mademoiselle?"

"Yes. I saw him—on the ground. He was all right," the girl added, dryly.

"You saw him after he left here!" exclaimed the countess. "I do not understand."

The girl saw she would have to go into particulars. But she did not tell the countess she had taken her trip to the field hospital with the secret agent, M. Lafrane.

"Dear me! That was so like him," the countess observed when she had heard the story of Aunt

Abelard and her pullets. "His brother, too——"

"Is Count Allaire like his brother?" Ruth asked quietly.

"Yes. In many ways."

"I have never seen a picture of the count, have I?" the American girl pursued.

"But, yes! You have but to look at Henri," laughed the countess. "A little older. Perhaps a little more serious of expression. But the same tall, slim, graceful figure, both. Pardon my pride in my sons, Mademoiselle. They are my all now. And they are both like me, I believe," she added softly.

Ruth looked at her with luminous eyes.

"Like you in every way, Madame? Given so entirely to the service of their country?"

"But yes! Too recklessly patriotic, I fear," said the countess. Then, with a start, she exclaimed: "What is this? Do my eyes deceive me? Is it that wicked Bubu, running wild and free again?"

Ruth turned quickly. Crossing the wide lawns she saw the greyhound pass swiftly. He was without his blanket, and it seemed to Ruth as though the barrel of his body was much lighter of color than his chest and legs. Like a flash he was behind the chateau.

"Ma foi!" gasped the countess. "What is—— Something——"

She started to follow the dog. As she still clung to Ruth's arm the girl must perforce go with her. Through Ruth's mind was swirling a multitude of suspicious thoughts.

CHAPTER XVI: THE HOLLOW TOOTH

Bubu had been running at large—and in the daytime. He had come from the north. Ruth believed the dog had crossed the lines and just now had arrived at the chateau after his long and perilous journey.

Yet for a greyhound the fifteen or twenty kilometers between the chateau and the battle front was a mere nothing. At the rate the girl had seen the "werwolf" flying over the fields, he must have covered that distance faster than an automobile. And, too, he would take a route much more direct.

The countess seemed to have forgotten Ruth's presence; but the girl could not well draw her arm away and remain behind. Besides, she was desperately eager to know what would be done to Bubu, or with him, now that he had returned to the chateau. It was not unwillingly that the girl accompanied the countess.

It was some distance around the great building to the rear. They came upon the excited Dolge and the big dog, the latter lapping water out of a pan near the well house.

"Non! non!" cried the countess warningly. "Not that, Dolge. He must not be allowed too much cold water after his so-exciting run. It is not good for him."

The gardener stooped to take the pan away, and the greyhound growled. "Oh, la, la!" mumbled Dolge. "Name of a mouse! Would you butcher me, you of bloody mind?"

Ruth noticed that the barrel of the greyhound was almost white, which assisted in giving him that ghostly appearance at night.

The countess left Ruth and hurried forward. She did not stoop, but with her foot she straightway overturned the pan, sending the water out on the stones.

The dog looked up at her, wide-mouthed and with tongue hanging. But he did not offer to molest her. He only dropped his head again, and with his pink tongue sought to lap up the moisture from the stones.

"The collar, Dolge," commanded Madame la Countess.

The old man hobbled forward with the wide leather strap attached to the chain. The strap was decorated with big brass rivet heads. She buckled it around the neck of the panting dog. He lapped her hands.

"Ah, naughty one," she murmured, "would you run the fields like a wild dog? The blanket, Dolge. He may take cold."

Already the gardener was bringing the covering. They fastened it about Bubu, who finally shook himself and would have lain down had not the countess said sharply:

"Nay, nay! All is not yet finished, Bubu. Open thy mouth—so!"

She forced open the big dog's jaws. Rather, at a touch he allowed her to hold his dripping jaws apart.

"Dolge!" she demanded decisively, "can you see?"

"Oui, oui, Madame!" the old man chattered, shaking his head vigorously. "But not for me will he keep his jaws apart. I am not to be made into sausage-meat, I hope?"

The countess laughed at him. "Hold his mouth open, then. He would not desire to bite; but——"

Ruth, amazed, saw her white fingers fumble inside the dog's open maw. She pulled what seemed to be a white rubber cap from one of his grinders. Quickly and skilfully, with a fine knitting needle, the countess ripped from this rubber casing what the girl thought looked like a twist of oiled paper.

"All right, my good Dolge. You may let him go," she said, hiding the twist of paper in her palm. "Let him rest—poor fellow!"

She patted the greyhound with the sole of her slipper and the big dog yawned; then laid his head upon his paws. He was still panting, his sides heaving heavily. His legs and feet were bedaubed with mud.

"He has come a long way," the countess said coolly to Ruth. "Let us go in, Mademoiselle. It must be that our tea is ready."

She seemed to consider Ruth quite worthy of her confidence. The American girl knew that she was on the verge of an important discovery. It could not be that Bubu carried messages to Germany to give aid and comfort to the enemy! That suspicion was put to rest.

Bubu was being used to bring news from French spies across the battle lines. Otherwise the countess would never have allowed Ruth to discover this mystery of the "werwolf."

And how shrewd was the method followed in the use of the obedient dog! A hollow tooth, which would be overlooked even if the enemy shot and examined the animal.

Ruth wanted to ask a hundred questions; but she did not open her lips It might be that the countess supposed she was already aware of the use made of Bubu, and how he was used. The American girl had been brought to the chateau by Monsieur Lafrane, the agent of the French secret service bureau. And the countess knew, of course, his business.

As soon as they were in the library, where the tea things were laid, the countess proceeded to smooth out the bit of paper and examine it under a strong reading glass.

"Ah!" she cried, in a moment, her smooth cheeks flushing and her eyes brightening. "He is well! My dear boy!"

Her joy urged Ruth to question her, yet the girl hesitated. Her eyes, however, revealed to the countess her consuming curiosity.

"Mademoiselle!" exclaimed the old lady, "do you not know?"

"I—I don't know what you mean, Madame," stammered Ruth.

"It is from the count—my Allaire!"

"The message is from Count Marchand?" cried the girl, in utter amazement.

"But yes. He does not forget his old mother. When able, he always sends me word of cheer. Of course," she added, looking at the American girl curiously now, "there is something else upon the paper. His message to his mother is not a line. You understand, do you not? Monsieur Lafrane, of course——"

"Monsieur Lafrane has never told me a word," Ruth hastened to say. "I only suspected before to-day that Bubu carried messages back and forth across the lines."

"Ah, but you are to be trusted," the countess said cheerfully. "We do what the Anglais call—how is it?—'our little bit'? Bubu and I. He, too, is French!" and she said it proudly.

"And for years, Mademoiselle, we have established this couriership of Bubu's." She laughed. "Do you know what the farmers say of our so-good dog?"

Ruth nodded. "I have heard the story of the werwolf. And, really, Madame, the look of him as he runs at night would frighten anybody. He is ghostly."

The countess nodded. "In that's his safety—and has been since before the war. For, know you, Mademoiselle, all France was not asleep during those pre-war years when the hateful Hun was preparing and preparing.

"My husband, Mademoiselle Fielding, was a loyal and a far-sighted man. He did not play politics, and seek to foment trouble for the Republic as so many of our old and noble families did. Now, thank heaven, they are among our most faithful workers for la patrie.

"But, see you, Count Marchand owned a small estate near Merz, which is just over the border in Germany. Sometimes he would go there—sometimes to drink the waters, for there are springs of note, perhaps for the hunting, for there is a great forest near. He would always take Bubu with him.

"And so we taught Bubu to run back and forth between here and there. He carried messages around his neck in those times. Quite simple and plain messages, had he been caught at the frontier and examined.

"It was our Henri who resorted to the hollow tooth, and that since the war began. Bubu had one big tooth with a spot on it. Henri knew an American dentist in Paris. Ah, what cannot these Americans do!" and the countess laughed.

"We took Bubu to Paris and had the decayed spot drilled out. The tooth is sound at the root. The dentist made the hole as large as possible and then we moulded the rubber caps to close it. You see how the messages are sent?"

"Remarkable, Madame!" murmured Ruth. "But?"

"Ah? Who sends the messages from beyond the German lines? Now it is Count Allaire himself," she hastened to explain. "In disguise he went through the lines some weeks ago. The agent who was there came under suspicion of the Germans."

"And he lives at the castle over there in Germany—openly?" gasped Ruth.

"Nay, nay! It is no castle at best," and the countess laughed. "It is by no means as great a place as this. It was a modest little house and is now the comfortable quarters of a fat old Prussian general.

"But upon the estate is the cottage of a loyal Frenchman. He was gardener there in my husband's time. But as he bears a German name and his wife is German, they have never suspected him.

"It is with this old gardener, Brodart, my son communicates; and it is to him our good Bubu goes."

"But how can the dog get across No Man's Land?" cried Ruth. "I do not understand that at all!"

"There are bare and bleak places between the lines which we know nothing about," the countess said, shaking her head. "Not in all places are the two armies facing each other at a distance of a few hundred yards. There is the lake and swampland of Savoie, for instance. A great space divides the trenches there—all of two miles. Patrols are continually passing to and fro by night there, and from both sides. A man can easily get through, let alone a dog.

"Hush!" she added, lowering her voice. "Of course, I fear nobody here now. Poor Bessie—who was faithful to me for so many years—was contaminated by German gold. But she was half German at best. It was well the poor soul escaped as she did.

"However, my remaining servants I can trust. Yet there are things one does not speak of, Mademoiselle. You understand? There are many good men and true who take their lives in their hands and go back and forth between the enemy's lines and our own. They offer their lives upon the altar of their country's need."

CHAPTER XVII: THE WORST IS TOLD

"But, Major Marchand? What of him?" Ruth asked, deeply interested in what the countess had said.

"He, too, is in the secret work," responded the countess, smiling faintly. "My older son claimed the right of undertaking the more perilous task. Likewise he was the more familiar with the vicinity of our summer estate at Merz, having been there often with his father."

"But Major Henri goes back and forth, along the front, both by flying machine and in other ways?" Ruth asked. "I am sure I have seen him——"

She wanted to tell the countess how she had misjudged the major. But she hesitated. There was the matter of Nicko, the chocolate peddler, and the man who looked like him!

Could that disguised man have been the major? And if so, what was his interest in the German officer who had so suddenly died in the field hospital—the occupant of Cot 24, Hut H?

The girl's mind was still in a whirl. Had she called Lafrane to the front for nothing at all? Had she really been stirring up a mare's nest? She listened, however, to the countess' further observations:

"But yes, Mademoiselle, we all do what we may. My sons are hard at work for la patrie—and brave Bubu!" and she laughed. "Of course your American soldiers cannot be expected to take over the scouting on this front, not altogether, for they do not know the country as do we French. Yet some of your young men, Henri tells me, show marvelous adaptability in the work. Is it the Red Indian blood in them, think you, that makes them so proficient in scouting?" she added innocently.

But Ruth did not laugh. Indeed, she felt very serious, for she was thinking of Tom Cameron. Major Henri Marchand must know about Tom—where he was and what he was doing. That is, if it had been the major who had dropped the message from Tom at her feet the day before.

She could not discuss this matter with the countess. And yet the girl was so troubled regarding Tom's affairs that she felt equal to almost any reckless attempt to gain information about him.

Before the girl could decide to speak, however, there was a step upon the bare floor of the great entrance hall of the chateau. The ringing step came nearer, and the countess raised her head.

"Henri! Come in! Come in!" she cried as the door opened.

Major Marchand marched into the room breezily, still in the dress uniform Ruth had seen at Aunt Abelard's cottage.

"Ah, Mademoiselle!" he cried, having kissed his mother's hand and suddenly beholding the girl who had shyly retired to the other side of the hearth. "May I greet you?"

He came around the tea table and took her hand. She did not withdraw it abruptly this time as he pressed his lips respectfully to her fingers. But she did blush under his admiring glance.

"See, Henri!" his mother cried. "It is the good Bubu who has brought it. In code. Can you read it?"

She thrust the whisp of paper, taken from the dog's hollow tooth, under his eyes before pouring his cup of tea. Henri, begging Ruth's indulgence with a look, sat down before the table, his sword clanking. He smoothed the paper out upon the board and drew the reading glass to him.

"Wait!" Countess Marchand said. "You have had no luncheon! You are hungry, my dear boy?"

She hurried out of the room intent upon her son's comfort. Ruth watched the countenance of the major as he read the code message. She saw his expression become both serious and troubled.

Suddenly he turned in his chair and looked at the American girl. His gaze seemed significant, and Ruth began to tremble.

"Mademoiselle?"

"Yes, Monsieur?"

"You have questions to ask me, hein?"

"It is true, Major Marchand," she murmured, struggling for self-control. "I am eaten up by curiosity."

"Is it only curiosity that troubles you, Mademoiselle?" he said dryly.

"No! No! I am seriously alarmed. I am anxious—for a friend." Her voice was tense.

"You received a certain message?" he asked.

"Oh, yes, Major Marchand! And that excites me," she replied, more calmly now. "Was it really you who dropped the paper bomb at my feet?"

His eyes danced for a moment. "That was entirely—what you call—by chance. Mademoiselle, I spied you, and having the written message of your friend I inserted it in the bomb, twisted the neck of it, and let it fall at your feet. You are, of course, acquainted with Lieutenant Cameron?"

"He is the twin brother of my dearest friend," Ruth replied. "Helen is in Paris—helping make soup for French orphans," and she smiled. "Something that I have heard has worried me vastly about Tom." Her smile disappeared and her gaze at the French major was pleading.

His own countenance again fell into serious lines, and he tapped the table thoughtfully. Ruth clasped her hands as she waited. She felt that something untoward was about to be made known to her. There was something about Tom which would shock her.

"I am sorry, Mademoiselle," murmured the major. "Here is something said about Lieutenant Cameron."

"In that message Bubu brought?" she asked slowly.

"Yes. It is from my brother. Did you know that Lieutenant Cameron was working with the Count Marchand in Germany?"

"Oh, I did not know it until—until lately! There are such stories afloat!"

"Ah!" He smiled and nodded understandingly. "Do not let those idle tales annoy you. Lieutenant Cameron is a very able and a very honorable young man. He volunteered for the dangerous service. Of course, his comrades could not be told the truth. And it chanced he was observed speaking to one of our agents who came from the German side.

"At once it was decided that he would do well in the area of Merz, where Count Marchand is in command. You understand? Lieutenant Cameron's comrades were given the wrong impression. Otherwise, knowledge that he was a scout might have been easily discovered by German spies in this sector. Your friend speaks perfect German."

"Oh, yes," Ruth said. "He began to prattle to Babette, his German-Swiss nurse when he was a child."

"So he has been of much help to us near Merz. But my brother informs me now that a serious difficulty has arisen."

"What is it, Major Marchand?" asked the girl, with tightening lips.

"Lieutenant Cameron has been arrested. He is suspected by the Germans at Merz. He was furnished the papers and uniform of a Bavarian captain. The authorities are making an investigation. It may—I am desolated to say it, Mademoiselle!—become fatal for Lieutenant Cameron."

CHAPTER XVIII: BEARING THE BURDEN

It was dusk before Ruth Fielding arrived at the Clair Hospital after her exciting call at the Chateau Marchand. She had refused to allow Major Marchand to accompany her to the village, for she learned he must be off for the front lines later in the evening, and would in any case have but a few hours with his mother.

Ruth had conceived a plan.

She had been in serious conference with Major Marchand and the countess. Neither, of course, knew the particulars of Tom Cameron's arrest at Merz, beyond the German lines. However, they sympathized with her and applauded her desire to help Tom.

For there was a chance for Ruth to aid the young American lieutenant. The major admitted it, and the countess admired Ruth's courage in suggesting it.

The brief announcement of Tom's arrest sent by Count Marchand by Bubu, the greyhound, together with facts that the major knew, aided Ruth in gaining a pretty clear understanding of Tom Cameron's situation.

He had volunteered for this dangerous service and had been assigned to work with the French secret agents on both sides of the battle line. After his own comrades' suspicion was fixed on him, it was decided, Tom agreeing, that he would be able to do better work in Germany. Major Marchand had himself guided the American lieutenant to Merz, and introduced him to Count Allaire Marchand.

"And we both consider him, Mademoiselle," said the major generously, "a most promising recruit. We arranged for him to enter Merz in the guise of a wealthy Bavarian Hauptman on leave. Merz, you must understand, was quite a famous health resort before the war. Many foreigners, as well as Germans, went there to drink the waters. That is why we had a summer estate on the outskirts of Merz."

In addition, the major told of Tom's early successes in getting acquainted with the chief men of the town—particularly with the gouty old Prussian general, who was the military governor of the district. Information which Tom had gained, the major whispered, had spurred the American authorities in this sector to remove the civilian population for several miles back of the trenches.

There was soon to be a "surprise" attack upon the Americans, and the huge guns being brought up for the bombardment before the infantry advance might utterly wreck the open country immediately back of the American trenches.

Tom Cameron, posing as Captain Von Brenner, was apparently awaiting at Merz's best hotel the appearance of his sister, who, he declared, would join him before the conclusion of his furlough. At first the old general and the other authorities had accepted the American at his face value.

Somehow, suspicion must have been aroused within the last twenty-four hours. The message that had come by Bubu stated that Tom was under arrest as a suspicious person, but that he was detained only in the general's quarters.

It was something that might blow over. Finesse was required. Ruth had suggested a plan, which, although applauded by the major and his mother, they could not advise her to carry out. For, if it failed, her own peril would be as great as Tom Cameron's. In fact, the result of failure would be that both of them would be shot!

But the American girl was inspired for the task. So, urged by the countess, her son had agreed to assist Ruth in an attempt which he could but approve. Had Count Allaire Marchand, or any of his French operatives in and near Merz, attempted to assist in Tom Cameron's escape out of Germany, they would merely lay themselves open to suspicion, and possibly to arrest.

Ruth saw a code message written to the count, who was hiding on what had been the Marchand estate before the war, and then saw Bubu called into the library and the twist of oiled paper secreted in the dog's mouth. When the greyhound was released for his return journey to Merz, Ruth, likewise, left the chateau. A short time later, as has been said, she arrived safely at the hospital in the village.

Just as she was about to enter the gateway, a heavy touring car rumbled up the road from the south. It stopped before the hospital gate. There was a uniformed officer on the seat beside the chauffeur; but the only occupants of the tonneau were two women.

"We wish to see Miss Fielding," said one of these women, rising and speaking hastily to the sentinel who had presented arms before the gateway.

"I shall have to call somebody from inside, Mademoiselle," said the old territorial who was on guard duty. "There is such a name here, I believe."

"Never mind calling anybody!" Ruth suddenly exclaimed, springing forward. "Miss Fielding is here to answer the call. Will you girls tell me what under the sun you have come here for? I thought you would know enough to remain safely in Paris!"

"Ruthie!" shrieked Helen Cameron, fairly throwing herself from the automobile into Ruth's arms. "It is she! It is her! It is her owniest, owniest self!"

"Hold on," said the second occupant of the automobile tonneau, alighting more heavily. "Leave a bit for me to fall on, Nell."

"Don't you dare, Heavy Stone!" cried Ruth. "If you fell upon my frailness——"

"Hush! Tell it not in Gath," cried Jennie sepulchrally. "I have lost flesh—positively."

"Yes," agreed Helen, quite dramatically. "She barked her knuckle. Every little bit counts with Heavy, you know."

Ruth welcomed the plump girl quite as warmly as she did her own particular chum. Immediately the military automobile rolled away. The visitors both carried handbags.

"How did you come to get here—and where under the sun will you stay?" Ruth demanded again.

"Now, never mind worrying about us, Martha," Jennie Stone returned. "We will get along very well. Isn't there a hotel?"

"A hotel? In Clair?" gasped the girl of the Red Mill. "I—should—say—not!"

"Very well, dear; we'll put up wherever you say," said Helen airily. "We know you are always a favorite wherever you go, and you must have loads of friends here by this time."

"The unqualified nerve of you!" gasped Ruth. "But come in. I'll speak to Madame la Directrice and see what can be done. But how did you ever get permission to come here?" she repeated.

"It is our furlough. We have earned it. Haven't you earned a furlough yet?" Helen demanded, making big eyes at her chum.

"It never crossed my mind to ask for one," admitted the girl of the Red Mill. "But merely your having a furlough would not have won you a visit so near the front."

"Really?" asked Jennie. "Do you mean to say this is near the battle line?"

"You'd think so at times," returned Ruth. "But answer me! How did you get your passports viséed for such a distance from Paris?"

"Forget not," said Jennie, "that Mr. Cameron was over here on Government business. Helen can do almost anything she likes with these French officials."

"Humph!" was all that came from Ruth in answer to this.

"You don't seem glad to see us at all, Ruthie Fielding!" cried Helen, as they crossed the courtyard and mounted the steps to the hospital.

But Ruth was frankly considering how she could make the best use of her two college chums, now that they were here. In less than twenty-four hours she expected to leave Clair for an extended absence. She had been troubled regarding her duty to the Red Cross.

Circumstances had played into her hands. She could trust Helen and Jennie to do her work here at the Clair Hospital while she was absent.

She found the matron and took her aside before introducing her to the newcomers. She did not explain her reason for wishing to absent herself from duty for some days, nor did the tactful Frenchwoman ask after she was told that the Countess Marchand approved. But she told the matron about her two girl friends who had arrived so unexpectedly.

"They are good girls, and capable girls, and I can show them very briefly my ordinary duties, Madame."

"It is well, Mademoiselle Fielding," the woman said with cordiality. "Let me now greet your friends."

So Helen and Jennie were introduced, and the matron said she would find two rooms in the nurses' quarters for the visitors. But first the three girls must go to Ruth's little cell and have tea while they talked.

"First of all," Helen began. "How is Tommy-boy?"

"He is perfectly well as far as I know," Ruth said gravely.

"Goodness! You are not mad with him?"

"Of course not. How silly," her chum returned.

"Well, but don't you see him every day or two?"

Ruth Fielding stared at her chum, not alone with gravity, but with scorn.

"I think it is well you have come up here to visit," she said. "Don't you know yet that we are in this war, Helen Cameron?"

"I don't know what you mean," returned Helen, pouting. "If we were not at war with Germany, do you think I would be away from Ardmore College at this time of year?"

"Tom is on active service," Ruth said quietly. "I am rather busily engaged myself. I have seen him just twice since I have been at Clair. But I happened to learn to-day that—beyond peradventure—he is in health."

"That's good enough!" exclaimed Helen. "And I suppose you can get word to him so he'll know Jennie and I are here?"

"I will try to get word to him," agreed Ruth soberly.

"He can ask off and come to see us, can't he?"

"Not being in military charge of this sector, I cannot tell you," the girl of the Red Mill said dryly. "But if you remain here long enough I hope Tom will come to see you, my dear."

She could tell them no more. Indeed, to-night she did not even wish the girls to know that she proposed absenting herself from the hospital for a time and expected Helen and Jennie to do her work.

She had a burden to shoulder that she could not share with her friends. She sent them to their beds a little later to sleep confidently and happily after their long journey from Paris.

As for Ruth Fielding, she scarcely closed her eyes that night.

CHAPTER XIX: ADVENTURE

In the dawn of the next morning Ruth arose and rearranged all her stock of supplies and corrected the schedule of goods on hand. Despite her recent activities she had kept her accounts up to date and every record was properly audited.

Before Helen Cameron and Jennie Stone even knew how Ruth proposed making use of them, the girl of the Red Mill had explained her plan fully to the matron. That the Americaine Mademoiselle was so friendly with the grand folk at the chateau rather awed the Frenchwoman. She could find no fault with anything Ruth did.

But there was a great outcry when, at breakfast, Ruth explained to Helen and Jennie that she was called away from the hospital on private and important business, and for several days.

"She's running away to be married!" gasped Jennie Stone. "Treason!"

"Your romantic imagination is ever on tap, isn't it, Heavy?" responded Ruth with scorn.

"That's all right," returned the plump girl sharply. "You look out for your brother Tom, Helen Cameron."

"But it may be one of these French officers," Helen said, with more mildness. "Some of them are awfully nice."

"Don't be ridiculous, girls!" Ruth observed.

"Really it isn't at all nice of you, my dear," her chum said.

"I'm not doing this because it is nice," flared Ruth, whose nerves were a little raw by now. "It is something I have to do."

"What, then?" demanded Jennie.

"I can't tell you! It is not my secret! If it were, don't you suppose I would take you both into my confidence?"

"I don't know about that," grumbled Jennie Stone.

"I had made arrangements to do this before you came," the girl of the Red Mill said, rather provoked. "You must take me at my word. I cannot do differently. I never told you girls a falsehood in my life."

"Goodness, Ruthie!" exclaimed Helen, with sudden good sense. "Say no more about it. Of course we know you would not desert us if it could be helped. If Tom would only come while you are gone——"

"I may be able to communicate with him," Ruth said, turning her head quickly so that her chum should not see her expression of countenance. "And there is something you girls can do for me while I am gone."

"I warrant!" groaned Jennie. "No rest for the wicked. Don't try to think up anything in the line of cooking for me, Ruthie Fielding, for I won't do it! I have come here to get away from cooking."

"Will you fast then, while you remain at Clair?" asked Ruth rather wickedly.

"Ow-wow!" shrieked the plump girl. "How you can twist a fellow's meaning around! No! I merely will not cook!"

"But she still hopes to eat," said Helen. "What is it you want of your poor slaves, Lady Ruth?"

"Do my work here while I'm gone. Look out for the supplies. I can break you both in this morning. I do not know just when I shall be called for——"

"By whom, pray?" put in the saucy Jennie drawlingly.

Ruth ignored the question. "You will not find this work difficult. And, as Jennie suggests, it will be a change."

"Good-night!" groaned Jennie.

"Don't lose heart, sister," said Helen cheerfully. "I understand that Ruth often goes into the wards and writes letters for the poor poilus, and feeds them canned peaches and soft puddings. Isn't that what you do, Ruthie?"

"Better not let me do that," grumbled Jennie. "I might be tempted to eat the goodies myself. I'll write the letters."

"Heaven help the home folks of the poor poilus, my dear," Helen responded. "Nobody—not even Madame Picolet—could ever read your written French."

"Well! I do declare!" exclaimed the fleshy girl, tossing her head. "I suppose the duty will devolve upon me to eat all the blessés' fancy food for them. Dear me, Ruthie Fielding! Don't stay long. For if you do I shall utterly ruin my figure."

It was very kind of the girls to agree to Ruth's suggestion, and she appreciated it. But she could not tell them anything about what she was to do while she was absent from the hospital.

Indeed, she barely knew herself what she would do—in detail, that is. She had put herself in the hands of Major Marchand and must wait to hear from him.

She dared not breathe to Helen a word of Tom's trouble. Nobody must know that she, Ruth, hoped in some way to aid him to escape from beyond the German lines.

It seemed almost impossible for a girl—any girl—to pass from one side of the battle front to the other. From the sea on the Belgian coast to the Alps the trenches ran in continuous lines. Division after division of Belgians, British and their colonial troops, French, and Americans held the trenches on this side, facing a great horde of Germans.

In places the huge guns stood so close together they all but touched. Beyond these were the front trenches, in which the sharpshooters and the machine-gun men watched the enemy. And beyond again were the listening posts and the wire entanglements.

How could a girl ever get through the jungle of barbed wire? And in places the Huns had strung live wires, carrying voltages strong enough to kill a man, just as they did along the borderland of Holland.

When Ruth thought of these things she lost hope. But she tried not to think at all. Major Marchand had bade her be of good hope.

She kept her mind occupied in showing the two girls their duties and in introducing them to such of the nurses and other workers as Ruth herself knew well.

It was rather late in the afternoon, and she had heard no word of the major, when Ruth and her two friends came out of a lower ward to the main entrance of the hospital just as an ambulance rolled in. Two of the brancardiers came out of the hospital and drew forth one stretcher on which a convalescent patient lay.

"Oh, the poor man!" murmured Helen. "What do they do with him now?"

"He has come in from a field hospital," began Ruth. And then she saw the face of the ambulance driver. "Oh, Charlie Bragg!" she called.

"What did I tell you?" said Jennie solemnly. "She knows 'em all. They grow on bushes around here, I warrant."

"They don't grow 'em like Charlie on bushes, I assure you," declared Ruth, laughing, and she ran down the steps to speak to the ambulance driver, for she saw that he wanted to say something to her.

"Miss Ruth, I was told to whisper something in your private ear, and when I have said it, you are to do it, instantly."

"Goodness! What do you mean, Charlie Bragg?" she gasped.

"Listen. Those two brancardiers are coming for the second man. When they start up the steps with him, you pop into the back of the ambulance."

"Why, Charlie!" she murmured in utter amazement.

"Are you going to do as you are told?" he demanded with much apparent fierceness.

"But the third man? You have another wounded man inside."

The stretcher-bearers slid the second convalescent out of the ambulance.

"Now!" whispered Charlie. "Do as you are told."

Half understanding, yet still much puzzled, the girl went around to the rear of the ambulance. It was half dark within, but she saw the man lying on the third stretcher, the one overhead, put out a hand and beckon her. She could see nothing of his face, his head was so much bandaged. One arm seemed strapped to his side, too.

The engine of the car began to purr. Charlie clashed the clutch. Ruth jumped upon the step, and then crept into the covered vehicle. The car leaped ahead.

She heard Jennie Stone exclaim in utter amazement:

"Well, what do you think of that? What did I tell you, Helen? She is actually running away."

In half a minute the ambulance was out of the courtyard and the dust of the village street wan rising behind it, as Charlie Bragg swung the car into high gear.

This was adventure, indeed!

CHAPTER XX: ON THE RAW EDGE OF NO MAN'S LAND

"Sit down, Mademoiselle," said a low voice. "There is a cushion yonder. Make no sound—at least, not until we are out of the village."

Ruth could only gasp. There was light enough under the ambulance roof for her to see the speaker creep down from the swinging stretcher. He moved very carefully, but his bandages were evidently camouflage.

The jouncing of the automobile made her uncomfortable. Charlie Bragg was driving at his usual reckless pace. Ruth did not even laugh over the surprise of Helen and Jennie at her departure. She was too deeply interested in the actions of the man with her in the ambulance.

He was unwinding the bandage that strapped his left arm to his side and, with gravity, removed the splints that had evidently been put in place by a professional hand.

His arm, however, was as well and strong as Ruth's own. She saw that he wore a familiar, patched, blue smock, baggy trousers, and wooden shoes. He began to look like the mysterious Nicko, the chocolate vender!

Then he unwrapped his head. There were yards of the gauze and padding. To believe his first appearance once might have thought that his jaw had been shot away.

But at last Ruth saw his unmarred face so clearly that she could no longer doubt his identity. It was Major Marchand. And yet, it was Nicko!

"Pardon, Mademoiselle," said the officer softly. "It is necessary that I go disguised at times. My poor friend, Nicko (perhaps you saw him at the field hospital to which you were assigned for a week?), allows me to dress like him and did, indeed, allow me to live in his house at times. Now he has been removed from his home and fields with the rest."

"I think I understand, Major Marchand," she answered.

"I was much interested in a wounded Uhlan captain who was in that hospital. He began by trying to bribe our poor Nicko, thinking the chocolate peddler too weak-minded to be patriotic. He was mistaken," and the major nodded. "Had the Uhlan not died of his wounds I believe I should have got something of moment from him."

Ruth shook her head and asked: "Where are you taking me? Oh! I thought Charlie would have us over then!"

The major smiled. "Our friend, Monsieur Bragg, is faithful and wise; but he drives like Jehu. I have engaged him to transport us a part of the way."

"Part of the way to where?"

"To where we are going," Major Marchand replied dryly enough.

"But I was not exactly prepared, Major Marchand," Ruth said. "I am not properly clothed. I wear slippers and I have no hat."

"Trouble not regarding that," he told her. "It would be impossible for you to take a wardrobe across No Man's Land. An outfit of proper clothing must be secured for you upon the other side."

"Will that be possible?"

"German women still dress in the mode, Mademoiselle. And the garments you wear at Merz must bear the labels of Berlin tradesmen."

"Goodness! I never thought of that," admitted Ruth.

"Somebody must think of all the details," he said gently. "My brother will attend to it all."

"Count Allaire?"

"Yes. He is a master of detail," and the major smiled and nodded.

"You speak as though I were sure of getting across," Ruth whispered.

"Have no doubt, Mademoiselle. We must get over. Doubt never won in a contest yet. Have courage."

After another minute of jouncing about in the furiously driven ambulance, the girl continued her questioning:

"What am I to do first?"

"Do as you are told," he smiled.

"We are going toward the front now? Yes? And at what part of the line can we cross?"

"There is but one place where it is possible for you to get over. It is at the Savoie Swamps. It is a wild and deserted place—has always been. There is a little lake much sought by fishermen in the summers before the war started. The shores immediately about it are always marshy. At this season they are inundated."

"Then, how am I to get through?"

"That you will be able to understand better when you are there," said the officer noncommittally.

"Is it open country?" she asked wonderingly. "Shall we be quite exposed?"

"Not at night," he returned grimly. "And it is partly forest covered, that morass. The guns have shattered the forest in places. But most of the huge shells which drop into the swamp never explode."

"Oh!"

"Yes. They are very, very dangerous—those duds. But they will not be our only peril in crossing. Have you a brave heart, Mademoiselle?"

"I am going to help Tom Cameron escape," she said firmly.

He bowed and said nothing more until she again spoke.

"I can see that it may be possible for a man to get through that swamp—or across the lake by boat. But how about me? My dress——"

"I am afraid we shall have to disguise you, Mademoiselle," Major Marchand said with one of his flashing smiles. "But do not take thought of it. All will be arranged."

This was comforting, but only to a slight degree. Ruth Fielding was not a person given to allowing things to take their course. She usually planned far ahead and "made things come her way."

She stared out rather stonily upon the landscape. Charlie was still driving at his maddest gait. They passed few houses, and those they did pass were deserted.

"Your Americans, Mademoiselle," said the major, "have prepared for the expected German advance with a completeness—yes! They have my admiration."

"But will the attack come?" she asked doubtfully.

"Surely. As I told you, Mademoiselle, we can thank your young friend, Lieutenant Cameron, for the warning. Through his advantage with General Stultz he gained such information. The High Command of the German Armies has planned this attack upon the first American-held trenches."

"Oh, what will they do to poor Tom if they are sure he is a spy?" murmured Ruth, for the moment breaking down.

"We will get there first," was the assurance given her.

"But his sister—Helen—— Think of it, Major Marchand! She has just arrived at Clair and awaits him there at the hospital. I have not dared tell her that Tom has been caught by the Germans."

"Fear not," he urged her. "There is yet hope."

But every now and then Ruth felt her courage melting. It seemed so impossible for her to do this great thing she had set out to do. She felt her limitations.

Yet it was not personal fear that troubled her. She would have pressed forward, even had she been obliged to essay the crossing of No Man's Land alone.

At last the jouncing ambulance came to a rocking halt.

"As far as I can take you folks in this old fliver, I guess," drawled Charlie Bragg. "An unhealthy looking place for a picnic."

He twisted around in his seat to look at Ruth. She smiled wanly at him, while the Major got down quickly and offered her his hand.

"Is it all right, Ruth?" Charlie whispered. "I don't know this French chap."

"Don't fear for me, Charlie dear," she returned. "He is Major Henri Marchand. I fancy he is high in the French Army. And I know his mother—a very lovely lady."

"Oh, all right," responded the boy shortly. "One of the family, as you might say? Take care of yourself. Haven't heard from Cameron, have you?"

"That is what I am here for," whispered Ruth. "I hope I shall hear of him soon."

"Well, best o' luck!" said Charlie Bragg, as Ruth followed the major out of the rear of the ambulance.

The evening was falling. They stood at the mouth of a wide gully up which the car could not have traveled. The latter turned in a swirl of dust and pounded back toward the rear. When it was out of sight and the noise of it had died away, there did not seem to be any other sound about them.

"Where are we?" asked Ruth.

"Let us see," returned Major Marchand cheerfully. "I think we shall find somebody up this way."

They walked up the gully some hundreds of yards until they finally came out upon a narrow plain at the top. On this mesa was a ruined dwelling of two stories and some shattered farm buildings.

"Halt!" was the sudden command.

A man in khaki appeared from a clump of trees near the house, advancing his rifle.

"Friends," said the major quietly.

"Advance one friend with the countersign."

Major Marchand stepped ahead of Ruth and whispered something to the sentinel.

"Guess it's all right, Boss," said the sentinel, who evidently had no French. "But you can't proceed in this direction."

"Why not, mon ami?"

"New orders. Something doing up front. Wait till my relief comes on in half an hour. Top-sergeant will tell you."

"But we must go forward," urged the major, rather vexed.

"Don't worry," advised the American. "General orders takes the 'must' out of mustard even, and don't you forget it. If you were a soldier, you'd learn that," and he chuckled. "Come on over to the dyke and sit down—you and the lady," and he favored Ruth with an admiring glance.

The American girl did not speak, and it was evident that the sentinel thought her French like her companion. The three strolled along to the grassy bank behind the trees and directly before the half-ruined house.

Shell fire had destroyed one end of it. But the other end wall was complete. On the second floor was a window. The lower sash was removed, but in the upper sash there were several small, unbroken panes of glass.

There was the smell of smoke in the air, and the two newcomers spied a little handful of fire blazing on a rock under the dyke. Here the sentinel had made his little camp, and it was evident that he had boiled coffee and toasted meat within the hour.

"Great housekeeping," he said, grinning. "When I get back home I guess my mother'll make me do all the kitchen work. Ain't war what General Sherman said it was—and then some?"

"But we wish to hurry on, Monsieur," said the major quietly.

"Nothing doing!" responded the sentinel. "I got particular orders not to let anybody pass—not even with the word. Just stick around a little while, you and the lady. Toppy'll be along soon."

Ruth wondered that the French officer did not reveal his identity. But she remained silent herself, knowing that Major Marchand must have good reason for not wishing his rank known.

"We got to watch this old ranch," continued the talkative sentinel, nodding toward the half-ruined dwelling. "Somebody thinks there's something besides cooties in it. Yep," as the major started and looked at him questioningly. "Spies. Those Dutchmen are mighty smart, they do say. I'm told they flash signals from that window up yonder clear across the swamps to the German lines. Now, when it gets dark——"

He nodded and pursed his lips. The major nodded in return. Ruth remained silent, but she was becoming nervous. While they were in action and going forward the suspense was not so hard to bear. But now she began to wonder how she was ever going to cross that morass the major had told her about. And half a hundred other difficulties paraded through her troubled mind.

They sat upon the bank, and waited. The sentinel continued to march up and down just the other side of the fire, occasionally throwing a remark at the major, but usually with his face turned toward the house, which was distant about five furlongs.

Suddenly Ruth observed that Major Marchand had in his palm a little round mirror. He seemed to be manipulating it to catch the firelight. Ruth saw in a moment what he was about.

The sentinel stopped in his beat with a smothered exclamation. His back was to them and he was staring up at the open window of the house.

There came a flash of light from the window—another! Like lightning the sentinel raised his rifle and fired pointblank into the opening on the second floor.

Then, with a shout, he dashed across the intervening space and disappeared within the house. Major Marchand seized Ruth's hand and rose to his feet.

CHAPTER XXI: A NIGHT TO BE REMEMBERED

"Come!" the French officer whispered. "Now is our chance."

"Oh!" Ruth murmured, scarcely understanding.

"Haste! He will be back in a minute," the officer said.

He helped her over the dyke, and, stooping, they ran away from the abandoned house from which the puzzled American sentinel thought he had seen a spy flashing a light signal to the enemy lines.

"Fortunately, I had a little mirror," murmured Major Marchand, as he and the girl hurried on through the dusk. "With it, you see, I flashed a reflection of the firelight upon the broken panes of that upper window. Our brave young American will discover his mistake before his relief comes. We could not wait for that. Nor could we easily explain to his top-sergeant why we wished to go forward."

"Oh!" murmured Ruth again. "In your work, Monsieur, I see you have to take chances with both sides."

"It is true. Our own friends must not suspect too much about us. The best spy, Mademoiselle, plays a lone hand. Come! This way. We must dodge these other sentinels."

It was evident that he knew the vicinity well. Beyond the mesa they descended through a grove of big trees, whose tops had been shot off by the German guns.

They traveled through the lowland swiftly but cautiously. Ruth could not see the way, and clung to Major Marchand's hand. But she tried to make no sound.

Once he drew her aside into a jungle of brush and they crouched there, completely hidden, while a file of soldiers marched by, their file leader flashing an electric torch to show the way.

"The relief," whispered Major Marchand, when they had gone. "They may be swarming down this hill after us in a few minutes."

The two hurried on. The keen feeling of peril and adventure gripped Ruth Fielding's soul. It was not with fear that she trembled now.

At length they halted in a pitch-black place, which might have been almost anything but the sheepfold Major Marchand told Ruth it was. He produced an officer's trench whistle and blew a long and peculiar blast on it.

"Now, hush!" he whispered. "It is against usage to use these whistles for anything but the command to go over the top at 'zero.' Necessity, however, Mademoiselle, knows no law."

They waited. Not a sound answered. There was no stir on any side of them. Ruth's fears seemed quenched entirely. Now a feeling of exultation gripped her. She was fairly into this adventure. It was too late to go back.

The major blew the whistle a second time and in the same way. Suddenly a dark figure loomed before them. There was a word In French spoken out of the darkness. It was not the password the Major had given the American sentinel.

"Come, Mademoiselle," said the major. "Give me your hand again."

Ruth's warm hand slipped confidently into his enclosing palm. The Frenchman's courtesy and unfailing gentleness had assured her that she was perfectly safe in his care.

They left the sheepfold, the second man, whoever he was, moving ahead to guide them. Even in the open it was now very dark. There was no moon, and the stars were faint and seemed very far away.

Finally Ruth saw that a ridge of land confronted them; but they did not climb its face. Instead, they followed a winding path along its foot, which soon, to the girl's amazement, became a tunnel. It was dimly lit with an electric bulb here and there along its winding length.

"Where are we?" she whispered to the major.

"This is the first approach-trench," he returned. "But silence, Mademoiselle. Your voice is not—well, it is not masculine."

She understood that she was not to attract attention. A woman in the trenches would, indeed, create both curiosity and remark.

The guide stopped within a few yards and sought out trench helmets that they all put on. When the strap was fastened under her chin Ruth almost laughed aloud. What would Helen and Jennie say if they could see her in this brand of millinery?

She controlled her laughter, however. Here, at the first cross-trench, stood a sentry who let them by when the ghostly leader of the trio, whose face she could not see at all, had whispered the password. Ruth walked between her two companions, and her dress was not noticed in the dark.

Soon they were out of the tunnels through the ridge. Later she learned that the ridge was honeycombed with them. The trench they entered was broader and open to the sky. And muddy!

She stepped once off the "duckboards" laid down in the middle of the passway and dipped half-way to her knee in the mire. She felt that if the major had not pulled her up quickly she might have sunk completely out of sight.

But she did not utter a sound. He whispered in her ear:

"I admire your courage, Mademoiselle. Just a short distance farther. Do not lose heart."

"I am just beginning to feel brave," she whispered in return.

Presently the leader stopped. They waited a moment while he fumbled along the boarded side of the trench. Then a plank slid back. It was the door of a dugout.

"This way, Major," the man said in French.

The major pushed Ruth through the narrow opening. The plank door was closed. It was a vile-smelling place.

A match was scratched, a tiny flame sprang up, and then there flared a candle—one of those trench candles made of rolled newspapers and paraffin. It illumined the dugout faintly.

There were bunks along the walls, and in the middle of the planked cave was a rustic table and two benches. Evidently the men who sometimes occupied this trench had spent their idle hours here. But to Ruth Fielding it seemed a fearful place in which to sleep, and eat, and loaf away the long hours of trench duty.

"All ready for us, Tremp?" asked Major Marchand of the man who had led them to this spot.

The American girl now saw that the man was a squat Frenchman in the horizon blue uniform of the infantry and with the bars of a sergeant. He was evidently one of the French officers assigned to teach the Americans in the trenches.

In his own tongue the man replied to his superior. He drew from one of the empty bunks two bulky bundles. The major shook them out and they proved to be two suits of rubber over-alls and boots together—a garment to be drawn on from the feet and fastened with buckled straps over the shoulders. They enclosed the whole body to the armpits in a waterproof garment.

"A complete disguise for you, Mademoiselle—with the helmet," Major Marchand suggested. "And a protection from the water."

"The water?" gasped Ruth.

"We have half a mile of morass to cross after we get out of the trenches," was the reply. "I am unable to carry you over that, pickaback. You will have to wade, Mademoiselle."

CHAPTER XXII: THROUGH THE GERMAN LINES

Perhaps this was the moment most trying for Ruth Fielding in all that long-to-be-remembered night. And the Frenchmen realized it.

Having come so far and already having endured so much, however, the girl of the Red Mill was of no mind to break down. But the thought introduced into her brain by Major Marchand's last words was troubling her.

As for roughing it in such an admirable garment as this rubber suit, Ruth was not at all distressed. She had camped out in the wilderness, ridden half-broken cow ponies on a Wyoming ranch, and gone fishing in an open boat. It was not the mannish dress that fretted her.

It was the suggestion of the long and arduous passage between the American trenches and the German trenches. What lay for her in that No Man's Land of which she had heard so much?

"I am ready," she said at length, and calmly. "Am I to remove my skirts?"

"Quite unnecessary, Mademoiselle," replied the major respectfully. "See! The garment is roomy. It was made, you may be sure, for a man of some size. Your skirts will ruffle up around you and help to keep you warm. At this time in the year the swamp water is as cold as the grave."

Without further question the girl stepped into the rubber suit. Sergeant Tremp helped to draw it up to her armpits, and then buckled it over her shoulders. He showed her, too, how to pull in the belt.

She immediately felt that she would be dry and warm in the suit. And, although the boots seemed loaded, she could walk quite well in them. Major Marchand gave her a pair of warm gloves, which she drew on, after tucking her hair up under her helmet all around.

The major thrust two automatic pistols into his belt. But he gave her a small electric torch to carry, warning her not to use it.

"Then why give it to me?" she asked.

"Ah, Mademoiselle! We might need it. Now—allons!"

Tremp slid the plank back, and they filed out into the trench after he had looked both ways to make sure that the coast was clear. Ruth wondered what would happen to them if they were caught by an American patrol? Perhaps be apprehended for the spies they were—only the Americans would think them spying for the Huns!

The major's hands were full. Before the candle had been put out Ruth had seen him pick up two gas-masks, and he carried these as they stumbled along the duckboards toward the next cross trench.

"Halt!"

A sibilant whisper. Sergeant Tremp muttered something in reply. The trio turned the corner and immediately it seemed they were at the back of the firing shelf where—every so far apart—the figures of riflemen stood waiting for any possible German attack. The men in the trenches at night are ever on the alert.

Nobody molested the girl and her companions. Indeed, it was too dark to see much in the trench. But the sergeant seemed to know his way about perfectly.

Little wonder in that. The French had dug these trenches and Sergeant Tremp knew them as he did the paths in the environs of his native village.

At a dark corner he clucked with his tongue and brought them to a halt.

"This is it, Major," he whispered, after peering about.

"Good!" ejaculated the officer softly. "Let me step ahead, Mademoiselle. Cling to my belt behind. Try to walk in my footsteps."

"Yes," she breathed.

Tremp seemed to melt into the darkness. Major Marchand turned at an abrupt angle and Ruth followed him as he had desired. She knew they were passing through a very narrow passage. The earth was scraped from the walls by their elbows and rattled down upon their feet.

The passage rose slightly. The bottom of the trench they had just left—the very front line—was all of thirty feet in depth at this point. This narrow tunnel was thrust out into No Man's Land and led to a listening post.

At least, so she supposed, and she was not mistaken. Nor was she mistaken in her supposition that Tremp was no longer with them. He was not prepared to cross the Savoie morass.

A breath of sweeter air blew upon Ruth's cheek.

"Down!" whispered the major. They almost crawled the final few yards.

There was a quick word spoken ahead and the clatter of arms. Major Marchand shrilled a whisper in reply.

"Come, my boy," he said aloud, turning to Ruth. "We must step out lively. It is nearing ten o'clock."

"So you take a friend to-night, do you, Major?" asked a good American voice—that of the officer in command of the listening post.

"Aye," was the reply. "A boy to help me bring home the fish I may catch."

There was a little laugh. Ruth felt herself in a tremor. She knew instinctively that it would never do for her sex to be discovered.

She was not discovered, however. They stood upon the surface. Major Marchand took her hand and led her quietly away. The earth about them looked gray; but the blackness of night wrapped them around. There was not a light to be seen.

She realized more by the sense of locality she possessed than by aught else that they were on the lowland far beyond that ridge through which they had first tunneled after Sergeant Tremp had joined them.

Her eyes grew accustomed to the darkness as they stumbled on. Below them and ahead, she occasionally caught the glint of water. It was a pool of considerable size. She believed it must be the small lake Major Marchand had spoken of.

Suddenly Ruth seized her companion's arm.

"There!" she whispered.

"What is it?" he asked in the same low tone.

"There are men. See them?"

"No, no, Mademoiselle," he told her with a small chuckle. "There are no men standing so boldly there. They are posts—posts to which our barbed-wire entanglements are fixed."

"Oh!" she breathed with relief.

"Be not alarmed——" He seized her shoulder as he spoke and so great was his sudden pressure on it that he carried her with him to the ground.

A shower of flare rockets had erupted from the German trenches. They sailed up over No Man's Land and burst, flooding acres of the rough ground with a white glare.

The major and Ruth lay flat upon the ground, and the girl knew enough not to move. Nor did she cry out. For five minutes the eruption lasted. Then all died down and there was no reply from the American side. Major Marchand chuckled.

"That was most unexpected, was it not, Mademoiselle? But have no fear. The first patrol has already been across here to the German wire entanglements to-night, and found nothing stirring. It is not yet that we shall run into Germans."

They arose, and the major led straight on again, slowly descending the easy slope of this hillside. Finally they reached a gaping hole. Ruth knew it must have been made by a shell. It was thirty feet or more across, and when they descended into it she found it to be fully twenty feet deep.

"Now you may show a flash of your light, Mademoiselle," the Frenchman advised her. "Thank you. Remove that casque you wear. These would attract much attention upon the German side. Here is a German helmet to take the place of the other. I cached them on a former trip. So! Now, over this way. On hands and knees, Mademoiselle."

She followed him, obeying his word. So they crept out of the marmite hole and up under the entanglement of wire. It was plain that this path had been used before.

Once clear of the barrier, they descended the last few steps to the shore of the lake. There was thick shrubbery here, but Major Marchand led through this to the narrow beach.

"Can it not be crossed by boat?" she whispered.

"This water can be seen from watchers of both armies. Its least disturbance—even that occasioned by a swimmer—would draw volleys of shots from Americans and Germans alike.

"Now, we follow along this narrow beach. Step in my track, if possible, Mademoiselle Fielding. And keep within touch of me."

They walked on steadily. Soon the track became soft and sticky. She sank ankle deep in mire. Then gradually the morass grew deeper and she was in mud and water up to her knees. Later she was plodding half-leg deep, panting deeply.

The Frenchman wished to get to a certain place before they halted. The girl was almost exhausted when the major leaped out upon a log and offered her his hand.

"Come up here, Mademoiselle," he whispered. "We shall be dry here—and we can rest."

She could not speak; but her breathing soon grew calmer. Major Marchand said, suddenly speaking in German:

"Forget your French, Fraulein—from this point on. The German tongue only for us."

"Oh! Are we near?" she asked, obeying him.

"Yes. Can you go on again?"

"At once," she declared with confidence.

They walked to the end of the long log. Stepping down, she found that the quagmire was not so deep. But for some minutes they continued to plow through it, but walking as softly as possible.

Ahead there was a flash of light. Ruth thought it might be another flare, and prepared to drop down in the mud.

But it was merely an electric torch. There were voices—rougher voices than those to which Ruth had been used. She caught German words.

Major Marchand drew her behind the huge trunk of a tree. There splashed past through the mud a file of bulky figures. When they had gone, her companion whispered to the girl:

"Fraulein, it is a patrol. We are in good season. Soon we shall be there."

She was soon able to walk beside him on higher ground. She saved her breath for continued exertion. They came to a wire entanglement somewhat similar to that on the American side of the morass. But here a narrow path had been opened for the patrol.

"Halt! Who goes there?" croaked the sentinel.

"Ein Freund!"

The major gave the reply in a guttural tone. He stepped forward and whispered to the sentinel. Evidently he had the password of the Germans, as he had had that of the Americans!

Ruth followed on through the wires. They crossed a narrow field and were again challenged. Here a sergeant was brought to confer with the disguised Frenchman. But it was all right. He and his companion were passed, and they were led on by the sergeant.

They went over several bridges which spanned the front trenches and then their escort left them. Major Marchand seized Ruth's hand and held it for a moment.

"Rejoice, Fraulein!" he whispered. "We are through the lines."

CHAPTER XXIII: THE GARDENER'S COT

Ruth Fielding thought afterward that Major Marchand must possess the eyes of a cat. And his sense of locality was as highly developed as that of a feline as well.

In the midst of the wood into which they had come out from the German trenches he discovered a path leading to a tiny hut, which seemed entirely surrounded by thick brush.

He left her waiting for a moment while he ventured within. Then he came to the door and touched Ruth's sleeve.

"I can never know who is waiting for me here," he whispered.

"Your brother?"

"No, no! Some day they will suspect—these Boches—and they will find my little lodge. You know, Fraulein, the pitcher that too often goes to the well is at last broken."

She understood his meaning. At last he would be caught. It was the fate of most spies.

He lit a smoky lamp; but it gave light enough for her to see that the hut was all but empty. It must have been a swineherd's cot at a pre-war date. There was a table, a sawed-off log for a chair, a cupboard hanging against the wall, and a heap of straw in a corner for a bed.

This he pushed aside until he revealed beneath it a box like a coffin, buried in the dirt floor. Its cover was hinged.

From this hidden receptacle he drew forth the complete uniform of a Uhlan lieutenant. "Turn your back for a little, Fraulein," he said softly. "I must make a small change in my toilet."

He removed the muddy rubber suit and the helmet. Likewise, the smock, and baggy trousers, like those worn by Nicko the chocolate peddler. In a trice he clothed himself from top to toe as a Uhlan full lieutenant. He stood before the small glass tacked in the corner and twirled and stiffened his mustache with pomatum. When he turned and strode before Ruth again he was the typical haughty martinet who demanded of the rank and file the goose-step and "right face salute" of the German army.

"For your protection, Fraulein," he said, stooping at the box again, "we must make a subaltern of you."

"Oh! I could never look like a boy," Ruth objected, shrinking as she saw the second uniform brought to light.

"For your protection," he said again. "A girl like you, Fraulein, would not have the chance of a rabbit among these Huns. They are not French," he added dryly. "I will step outside. Make haste, please."

He practically commanded her to don the uniform he laid out.

Ruth let fall the heavy rubber garment she had worn through the swamp. Then she removed her outer clothing and got into the uniform and into the long, polished boots quickly. There was even the swagger cane that young Prussian officers carry.

She viewed herself as well as she could in the piece of mirror in the corner. She might have the appearance of a "stage" soldier; but nobody would ever, for a moment, take her for a man!

She strode up and down the hut for several moments, trying to tune her gait to her new character—no easy matter. Finally she went to the door. The lamplight showed her figure boldly in the frame of the doorway. She saw the waiting major start, and he muttered something under his breath.

"Am I not all right?" she asked with some trepidation.

For once Major Marchand forgot himself.

He bowed his stiff, military bow with a gesture as though he would kiss her finger tips.

"Assuredly, Mademoiselle!"

She drew back for him to enter the hut again. He withdrew from the box under the straw a long, military cloak, which he fastened upon Ruth's shoulders.

"It will cover the figure, Fraulein. And now, a bit of camouflage."

From his pocket he drew a leather roll, which, when opened, proved to contain shaving materials and certain toilet requisites. With a camel's hair brush dipped in grease paint he darkened her lip and her cheekbones just before her ears—as though the down of immature manhood were sprouting. She again looked at herself in the glass.

"I am a boy now!" she cried.

Major Marchand chuckled as he tumbled the rubber suits and all the other articles into the box, shut the cover and covered it with the straw. He looked carefully about the hut before they departed to make sure that no signs of their occupancy of it were left. He even rubbed out faint imprints of Ruth's slippers upon the damp earthen floor of the hut.

Putting out the smoky lamp, they left the place. The Frenchman seemed to know the vicinity perfectly. They followed yet another path out of the wood and came to what was evidently a small inn. There was a noisy party within, caparisoned horses held by orderlies in the yard, and several automobiles under the sheds.

"Some of the Crown Prince's wild friends," whispered Major Marchand to Ruth. "We must keep out of their sight but appear to be members of the party. Remember, you are Sub-Leutnant Louden. I am your superior, Leutnant Gilder. Do not speak if you can help it, Fraulein—and then of the briefest."

She nodded, quite understanding his warning. She was alive to the peril she faced, but she felt no panic of fright now that she was in the midst of the adventure.

The major found somebody in authority. An auto-car for hire? Surely! A price asked for it and a driver to Merz, which staggered Ruth. But her companion agreed with a nod. To be a Prussian lieutenant of the Crown Prince's suite one must throw money around!

In ten minutes they were under way—as easily as that was it accomplished. Huddled down in her corner of the tonneau, with the cloak wrapped around her, Ruth dozed. It was growing very late, and after her struggle across the swampland between the lines she was exhausted in body if not in mind.

She awoke suddenly. The car was stopping at a wide gateway and two sentries were approaching to examine their papers.

The Frenchman seemed prepared for everything. He had papers for himself and for "Sub-Leutnant Louden."

"Correct, Herr Leutnant. Pass on."

The car entered the private estate, but swiftly sped off into a side road instead of going up to the big house in the upper windows of which Ruth saw lights, although it was now nearly morning.

"Our quarters are in the gardener's cottage," said the major, loudly, evidently intending the information for the automobile driver's ear.

They came to a roomy old cottage. Its windows were dark. The chauffeur stopped before it and the major sprang out.

"Have a care how you step," he whispered to Ruth, and she made ready to get out of the car without a tumble. The high boots did feel queer on her legs.

Her companion was hammering on the door of the cottage with the hilt of his sword. A window opened above.

"Leutnant Gilder and Sub-Leutnant Louden billeted here. Make haste and come down," he commanded in his gruffest voice as the automobile wheeled around in the drive and started back for the gate.

In three minutes the door was opened; but it was dark inside.

"Is it thou, my Henri?" whispered a voice.

"Allaire!"

Ruth knew that it was the young count himself. Major Marchand drew her into the tiny hall. There was not much light, but she saw the two tall men greet each other warmly—in true French fashion—with a kiss upon either cheek.

CHAPTER XXIV: CAPTAIN VON BRENNER'S SISTER

The major turned immediately to Ruth, drawing his brother forward.

"Mademoiselle Ruth Fielding, Allaire. The Count Marchand," he whispered formally. "You understand, from my message by Bubu, Allaire, for what reason the lady has taken this arduous journey, do you not?"

"But yes," rejoined his brother. "Bubu safely arrived. I have not yet sent him back."

"But Tom—Lieutenant Cameron? What of him?" Ruth asked anxiously.

"Have no present fear, Fraulein," said the count in German. "He has not yet been allowed to return to his rooms at the hotel in Merz. That is all."

"He is a prisoner at the house up yonder, yes?" the major asked, with a shrug.

"Not a prisoner. A guest," replied the count. "General Stultz is still friendly. The Hauptman von Brenner," and he smiled, "is teaching the general some American card game, I believe. The whole staff is card-crazy. They have little else to do but play."

"And what plans have you already made for Fraulein Ruth?" queried Major Marchand.

"While she remains under this roof she will pass as Frau Krause's niece. But in the morning she will be furnished an outfit I have secured, and she shall enter Merz as a very different person."

"Oh, dear!" murmured Ruth. "Another disguise?"

"You could scarcely continue in your present dress and escape discovery—by daylight," the count said dryly.

This fact was, of course, patent. Ruth was only too glad that the voluminous cloak covered her completely.

The count led her up two flights of stairs to a tiny, neat chamber under the roof. It was evidently a domestic's bedroom.

"Put the uniform outside the door, Fraulein, when you remove it. It must be hidden," whispered the count. "You will find night apparel on the chair. The good Frau Krause has thought of everything."

This, indeed, seemed to be the fact when Ruth awoke from her sound sleep at mid-forenoon. She might not have aroused then had there not been an insistent tapping on the door.

"Ja? Herein!" exclaimed Ruth, not too sleepy to remember her German.

A broad face surmounted by a cap, then the woman—quite a motherly looking person—appeared. "I am to help the Fraulein dress," announced Frau Krause, smiling.

"If you will be so kind," the girl agreed.

What she had not noticed when she went to bed was an open trunk heaped with clothing—both for under and outer wear. The rich and "stuffy" gown was typically German, and so was the plumed hat.

Ruth was sitting, with her hat on, in the little dining-room of the cottage over her pot of substitute coffee, rye bread and schmierkäse, when a private and almost noiseless auto-car rolled up to the door. She went out and entered it quite alone, and they were out of the Marchand estate by a rear exit and on the highway to Merz before Ruth discovered that the capped and goggled chauffeur was none other than Count Allaire Marchand himself.

In a stretch of the road where there was no traffic and few houses in sight, he half turned in his seat and told Ruth in brisk, illuminating sentences what she was to do.

It sounded easy, providing she aroused no suspicion in the breasts of those whom she met. The supposed character of Captain von Brenner's sister would enable her to treat everybody in a distant and haughty manner.

"But be careful of your German, Fraulein," urged the count. "Make no error in your speech. Deny yourself to everybody until your brother appears. After your first outburst of anger and alarm, when you arrive at the hotel, retire to the rooms he engaged for you, and refuse to discuss the matter with anybody.

"It is, as you Americans say, one grand game of bluff. It can be carried through by no other means. Remember what I have told you to tell your brother. To-night at nine, or to-morrow night at nine, I will be in waiting with the car. This is absolutely all my brother and I can do for you."

In a few minutes the car rolled into the principal street of Merz. Just beyond the great, glass-roofed building, wherein in happier times the visitors went daily to drink the medicated waters, was the hotel.

A rheumatic old woman with a sash, who acted as carriage opener, with a young boy for porter, met "Captain von Brenner's sister." In the hall the corpulent host bowed before her.

"Captain von Brenner?" queried Ruth. "I am his sister."

Mine host paled. His eyes grew round with wonder.

"What it the matter with you?" asked the girl impatiently. "Are you dumb?"

"He is not here, mein Fraulein," chattered the man.

"Send for him, then. And show me to the suite he engaged for me."

"Fraulein! Pardon!" gasped the innkeeper. "We did not understand. That is—it was—— We thought he would not return."

"What?"

"And that—that the gnädiges Fraulein would not come."

"Idiot!" exclaimed Ruth, revealing an excellent semblance of rage. "You have relet my rooms?"

"But you may occupy the Herr Hauptman's," burst out the browbeaten Innkeeper.

"And where is Captain von Brenner?"

It all came out at one gush of chattering information. The captain had been sent for by the Herr General Stultz. He had already been away three days. It was whispered he was arrested.

After her first show of annoyance Ruth seemed to recover her self-possession. She listened more quietly to the explanation of the excited hotel man. Then she demanded to be shown to her "brother's" rooms.

There she sat down and wrote quite a long letter to Tom Cameron in the character of his sister, "Mina von Brenner." She was sure Tom would recognize her handwriting and understand at once that she was at Merz in an attempt to aid him.

"Fear not for me, Brother," she wrote in conclusion. "But hasten to assure your Mina that you are perfectly safe. Is it not possible for you to return to the hotel by dinner time? I am distraught for your safety."

She sent this letter, with gold, by the hotel keeper, who said he could find a messenger to go to the Marchand estate. Ruth knew, of course, that her letter would be read there before it was given to Tom.

Even if they questioned him about his sister before giving him the letter Tom would make no mistake. "Mina von Brenner" was already a character and name chosen by Count Allaire and Tom when the latter took up his difficult and dangerous work in the guise of an Uhlan captain.

That was one of the longest days Ruth Fielding had ever spent. As the hours dragged by she sat and pondered in the rooms Tom had occupied, one moment in despair of his coming, the next fearing that every step in the corridor outside her door was that of a guard come to arrest her.

Yet her own safety scarcely mattered. She felt that if she could not compass Tom's escape, she did not care to go back across the lines, were that even possible!

Ruth Fielding learned much about her own heart during that long wait—much that she would not have acknowledged to any other soul in the world.

It finally grew dark. She would allow the servant to light but a single candle. This stood upon her table beside which she sat with her forehead resting in her hand, her elbow on the table.

Suddenly there sounded a quick step in the corridor. Ruth had been mistaken so many times that she did not raise her head or look up. A rap on the door, and before she could say "Herein!" the knob turned.

A figure dashed in—a brave figure in a uniform somewhat similar to the one Ruth herself had worn the night before.

"Mina!" cried a welcome and familiar voice. "My dear sister!"

Tom rushed across the room. Ruth saw, as she rose, that there were two officers with him, but they remained outside. They saw Tom take her in his arms in a most affectionate and brotherly manner. Then they closed the door, evidently satisfied.

"No need of tearing my hair down and breaking my ribs, Tom," Ruth whispered. "Please remember that I am not Helen, after all."

"No," he returned softly. Then, holding her off to look more closely at her, he went on more lightly: "You are Mina von Brenner. Great heavens, my dear! How did you get here?"

CHAPTER XXV: BACK AGAIN

It was Ruth who finally remembered to order dinner sent up.

Her letter, read, of course, by the mildly suspicious old general, had served to release Tom from present espionage. There was not even a guard in the corridor when, just before nine, the "brother and sister" left the rooms and strolled out of the hotel into the streets.

They walked several blocks until Tom was assured they were not spied upon. Then quickly, through several short but crooked side streets, he led Ruth to a garage in an alley. He tapped a signal on the door. The latter slid back.

The purring of a motor was heard. A man silently got into the driver's seat. Tom helped Ruth into the tonneau and got in himself.

"You have your papers, Captain?" asked the count softly.

"Yes. They did not take them from me."

"And the lady's?" said the other. "If we are halted you know what to say?"

"Quite," returned Tom in German.

The car rolled out of the garage, the door of which closed as silently behind them as it had opened. Ruth made up her mind that Merz was quite as infested with French spies as the towns behind the French lines were infested with those of the Germans.

The car left the town quickly. She remembered the road over which she had traveled that morning. They entered the Marchand estate by the same rear gate where only one sleepy guard hailed them and did not even look at the papers when he observed Tom's uniform.

"Farewell," whispered the count as they approached the gardener's cottage. "I may not see you soon again, Captain. Nor the Fraulein. Best of luck!"

They alighted. The car wheeled and was gone. Good Frau Krause met Ruth at the door, hurried her up to the small room and there helped her into the uniform of the sub-lieutenant of Uhlans.

When Ruth came down into the parlor of the cottage she found two other officers of apparently her own regiment awaiting her. Tom rushed to her. But she only gave him her hand.

"Manifestly this is no place for renewed protestations of brotherly regard, Tommy," she said demurely. "I presume we have to go through all the difficulties we did last night, Major?"

"And quickly," muttered Major Henri Marchand, looking away from them. "There is something on foot. I should not be surprised if the promised attack and advance under barrage fire is to begin before morning."

"I am ready," the girl said simply.

"Here is the car I sent for," the Frenchman said, raising his hand as he heard the automobile without. "You ahead, Captain. Remember, you are our superior officer."

They filed out. The car which the major and Ruth had used in reaching the gardener's cottage from the German front stood panting on the drive. The three got in.

They wheeled around, boldly passing the front of the Marchand house where the general and his staff lived and where Tom had been an unwilling guest for three days, and so reached the main entrance of the estate.

Here their papers were scrutinized, but superficially. Captain von Brenner's name was already known. Leutnant Gilder and Sub-Leutnant Louden were remembered from the previous evening.

The car started again. It slipped between the massive stone posts of the gateway. It sped toward the front. But all the peril was yet ahead.

"How can we get through the German trenches if they are already filled with the shock troops that will be sent over following the barrage?" asked Tom.

"We must beat them to it, as you Americans say," chuckled the major, whose spirits seemed to rise as the peril increased.

And he prophesied well in this matter. They were, indeed, in the trenches before the reserves were brought up for the planned attack upon the American lines.

The trio of fugitives left the car at the wayside inn. They found the hidden hut and made their changes into rubber suits, an outfit being produced for Tom by the indefatigable Major Marchand.

Through the shrouding darkness they went in single file to the wood directly behind the trenches. As on the previous night the French spy had secured the password. Three men with an evident objective "up front" were allowed to pass without question.

Once "over the top" they lay in the field until a patrol went out through the wire entanglements to spy about No Man's Land. The three joined this party, but quite unknown to its leader.

Once on the black waste at the edge of the morass, the three fugitives separated from the German patrol and slipped down into the low ground. Major Marchand found the path, and, for a second time, there began for Ruth that wearisome and exhausting journey through the swamp.

This time, what with her failing strength and the excitement of the venture, Ruth was utterly played out when they reached the log whereon she and the major had rested the night before.

"We'll carry her between us—chair fashion," suggested Tom Cameron. "That is the way, Major. Interlock your hands with mine. Lean back, Ruthie. We'll get you out of this all right."

It was a three-hour trip to the American trenches, however, and, after a while, Ruth insisted upon being set down. She did not want to overburden her two companions.

At the listening post an officer was sent for who recognized Major Marchand and who took Tom and Ruth "on trust." The major, too, sent the word up and down the trenches by telephone that the expected advance of the Germans was about to occur.

As the three passed through the American lines, after removing the rubber suits in the dugout, they passed company after company of American troops marching into the trenches.

Tom left Ruth and the major at a certain place to report to his commander. But he promised to be in Clair the next morning to satisfy Helen of his safety.

It was almost morning before the major and Ruth secured transportation, the one to the Clair Hospital, the other to the chateau on the hill behind the village. But it was an officer's car they used, and it covered the distance less bumpily than had Charlie Bragg's ambulance.

"Mademoiselle," said Major Henri Marchand in his most punctilious way, "it is in my heart to say much to you. I approve of you—I admire you. Your courage is sublime—and your modesty and goodness equally so.

"Forgive the warm expressions of a Frenchman who appreciates your attributes of character, as well as your graces of person. Believe me your friend forever—your devoted and humble friend. And I trust your future will be as bright as you deserve."

The day was just breaking as he thus bade her good-bye and Ruth Fielding alighted from the machine at the gateway of the hospital.

She stood for a minute and watched the car disappear in the semi-darkness with this faithful soldier of France sitting so upright upon the rear seat. And she had once suspected him of disloyalty!

The sentinel presented arms as she went in. She climbed wearily to her own little white cell that looked out toward the battle front. Already the guns had begun—the big German guns, heralding an attack for which the Americans were prepared, thanks to Tom Cameron!

The thundering echoes awoke Helen and Jennie. They scurried into Ruth's little room to find her sitting on the side of her cot sipping hot tea which she had made over her alcohol lamp.

"Where have you been?" cried Helen. And Jennie chimed in with:

"Two whole nights and a day! It is disgraceful! Oh, Ruthie! Are you really wedded?"

"I am wedded to my work," replied the girl of the Red Mill quietly.

"Dear, dear! How original!" drawled Jennie.

"What are those guns?" demanded Helen. "Aren't they going to stop pretty soon?"

"They have merely begun. You are here in time to witness—from a perfectly safe distance—a German drive. This sector will be plowed by huge shells, and our brave boys in khaki will hold the German horde back. It will be one of the hottest contested battles our boys have experienced."

"Pooh! How do you know?" scoffed Helen.

"I warrant it will all be over in an hour," added Jennie. "What do you know about it, Ruth Fielding? You haven't been over there to find out what is in the mind of the Hun."

"Haven't I?"

Ruth Fielding hesitated. Should she tell them? What would these, her two closest girl friends, say or think, if they knew what she had been through during the past thirty-six hours?

Suppose she should picture her adventure to them—just as it had happened? Suppose she told them of her long journey with the French major across No Man's Land?

"Where is Tom? Did you get word to him?" Helen asked.

"He will be here this morning to see you," Ruth said, and then went back to her thoughts of her adventure.

"Goody! Dear old Tom will take us around and show us the big shell holes—and all," Helen declared.

Shell holes! Ruth remembered the shell hole in which they had changed steel helmets before and after crossing the swamp. How she must have looked in that shapeless rubber garment and steel hat!

"What under the sun are you laughing at, Ruth Fielding?" demanded Helen.

"Yes. Do tell us the joke," drawled Heavy Stone.

"I—I was ju-just thinking of how fun-funny I must ha-have looked in a hat I had on since I saw you girls!" Ruth was hysterical.

"Well! I never!" gasped Jennie.

"Dear me, Ruth," Helen said, admonishingly. "I wonder you are so light-minded at such a time as this. You are laughing when those horrid guns may be throwing shells right among our poor boys. Dear, dear! I wish they would stop."

Ruth gazed at Helen with a far-away look in her eyes.

"I'm not laughing," she said slowly. "Far from it!"

"Yes, but you did laugh!" burst out Jennie.

"If I did, I didn't know it," answered Ruth. "I was thinking of something else. Oh, girls, not now—to-morrow, perhaps—you may know about it. Now I'm tired, so tired!"

The two girls, at last realizing that something out of the ordinary had occurred and seeing how near the end of her strength Ruth really was, petted her, made her as comfortable as possible, and finally left her to rest, telling her they would still take charge of the supply room, so that the girl of the Red Mill need not take up at once her duties in the hospital.

THE END

Made in the USA
Monee, IL
15 November 2023

46570794R00056